MIXING SOME NITRO PUNCH!

Longarm rose to a half-crouch, enough to see the band of men as they were starting to pass the butte. He let them pass it by about fifty yards, and then with a prayer in his heart, pulled back the pouch of the slingshot as far as the rubber would stretch. Then, with as gentle a motion as he could, he released it. The glass vial flew through the Y of the slingshot and arced through the air. Both Longarm and Fisher watched in fascination as the vial arced further and further out . . .

An instant later there came a terrific explosion right in front of the charging gang of bandits. A cloud of smoke and dust and dirt went up. They could see the flash of fire at its center following the thunder-clap of the explosion, could hear the high whinnies of the horses and the shouts and curses of the men. Immediately several horses and a like number of men were down.

"My God," said Fisher. "Would you look at that . . ."

DON'T MISS THESE
ALL-ACTION WESTERN SERIES
FROM THE BERKLEY PUBLISHING GROUP

TABOR EVANS

LONGARM

AND THE
SILVER MINE MARAUDERS

J

JOVE BOOKS, NEW YORK

LONGARM AND THE SILVER MINE MARAUDERS

A Jove Book / published by arrangement with
the author

PRINTING HISTORY
Jove edition / May 1995

ISBN: 0-515-11612-2

A JOVE BOOK®
Jove Books are published by The Berkley Publishing Group,
200 Madison Avenue, New York, New York 10016.
JOVE and the "J" design are trademarks
belonging to Jove Publications, Inc.

PRINTED IN THE UNITED STATES OF AMERICA

10 9 8 7 6 5 4 3 2 1

Chapter 1

Deputy United States Marshal Custis Long was doing something he very seldom had the chance to do. He was doing nothing and taking quite a bit of enjoyment out of it. At that moment, he was lying on the bed in his room at the Grand Hotel in Taos, New Mexico, on a leave of absence, reflecting on the fact that he was in a hotel that had burdened itself with a name it couldn't possibly live up to.

But then Longarm really didn't care. It was late spring, the weather pleasantly warm during the day, the nights velvet with just a touch of ice for variety to make for good sleeping. He was taking a month of leave, something he did so seldom that he couldn't remember the last real rest he'd had. Normally his boss, Billy Vail, chief marshal in the Denver, Colorado, headquarters, was able to persuade Longarm to do "just one more job" before any kind of leave. In fact, Longarm had known years to go by that way.

But, after a particularly rough winter job in the mountains around Durango, Colorado, where he had come as close to freezing to death as he had ever expected to do,

Longarm had marched into Billy's office and announced that he was taking time off he was due and that Billy and the marshals service could be hanged for all he cared.

Surprisingly, Billy had given in with barely a whimper. In fact, he'd had the gall to say solicitously, "Well, Custis, I think it's about time that you took a leave. My God, a man can only do so much. You know, you ain't getting any younger, Custis, and you have to look out for yourself. You've been pushing yourself way too hard lately."

Longarm had stood there staring at Billy Vail. He'd been flabbergasted at the old hypocrite. So flabbergasted that he'd been unable to reply in kind with the same degree of hypocrisy. Instead, Longarm had said, "Consider me gone." He'd turned on his heels and walked out of the office to leave word where his mail and any messages could be forwarded and where he could be reached in case of an emergency.

He'd also told the clerk at the administration office that it had better be a damn large emergency before anybody tried to reach him. He'd said, "The first time anybody puts out a hand toward me, they're liable to draw it back missing a few fingers."

He'd chosen Taos because it had warmer weather, there were some serious poker players in the town, there was horse racing, and there was always an excellent chance for female companionship of the willing persuasion. He liked the Grand Hotel because of the big thick adobe brick walls. It was cool in the day, and they gave you plenty of blankets at night. The food in the dining room was good and they had a first-class saloon where well-heeled poker players tended to show up. Longarm liked the town. It was old, and it had once been the site of the headquarters of the Taos Indian tribe, but they had long been scattered like most of the New Mexico cave-dwelling Indians. Taos itself

2

sat down in a little valley, surrounded by some fair hills and mountains. Now it was greening up, and would be ripe and lush within another couple of weeks. Longarm had every intention of spending his thirty-day leave without ever getting astride a horse to go anywhere at all, except to the fairgrounds near the edge of town to watch the horse racing and maybe bet a few dollars.

Longarm had been there a week and was utterly content with life. He lay on the bed now with only his jeans on. He wasn't a man who much cared for underwear except in the coldest of weather. He was of the opinion that it slowed a man down if a willing woman came along. Now it was a comfort to laze around without a care in the world, to take a delicate sip of the Maryland whiskey that he preferred—of which he had brought a fair supply—to eat when he felt like it, to get plenty of sleep, and to let the world look after itself for a change.

No one, except for his boss, called him Custis. Most people knew him by his nickname, Longarm. He had gotten that because of a combination of his last name, Long, and the fact that Billy Vail delighted in sending him to hell and back after whatever criminal or desperado Billy decided needed apprehending the most at any particular time. Hence had come Longarm, the long arm of the law. He didn't much care for it himself, but there wasn't anything he could do about it, so he generally answered to it when he was called.

Looking at him, you would say he was of an indeterminate age. His weathered face was marked by cold winds and hot summers, sandstorms and blizzards, and lined with worry and concern and fatigue and desperation. It could have been the face of a man at least forty, but his strong muscular body with his big arms, shoulders, and hands was more like that of someone in their thirties. He was about six feet tall, although he wasn't sure exactly because he had never taken the trouble to measure himself. He weighed, depending on how he had been eating, somewhere around 190 pounds. He had a friendly face and hazel blue eyes that could go agate-hard on certain occasions.

Longarm was a deputy United States marshal, both by vocation and by conviction. He was a sincerely honest man who cared about his neighbor and who did not at all care for people who broke the law or who would harm those weaker than themselves. He was relentless in pursuit, merciless in a fight, and never willing to concede defeat so long as he was still breathing. Criminals and bandits and desperados knew him from the badlands of Kansas to the Mexican border in Texas, in Arkansas and Louisiana in the east, and in Arizona and New Mexico and Nevada in the west. There was nowhere he would not pursue wrongdoers, and once on that trail he would not stop until justice, in whatever form it took, had been done. He had fears, he was mortal, but they never showed. They only took their toll inside. Longarm was a man who, in the right circumstances, laughed easily, liked a good time, loved women, liked to gamble, loved to trade horses. But he loved his job more than anything else.

But sometimes he had to have a rest, and this was one of those times. It was with luxurious delight that he contemplated three more weeks of lying around, drinking and gambling, and satisfying to the best of his ability whatever female companionship chance might throw his way.

He sat up on the side of the bed, deciding that it was time for an afternoon drink. He poured out three fingers of the Maryland whiskey into a mostly clean glass, and was on the point of sipping it when there came a light rapping at his door.

He put the glass down on the bedside table and curled his fingers around the butt of his .44-caliber Colt revolver. He might be on vacation, but he still had plenty of enemies who weren't.

Over his shoulder he asked, "Who is it?"

He heard muffled words that he could not distinguish. He said, "Come in!" and drew the revolver partway out of the holster. He turned around to see it was one of the young boys who worked around the hotel.

Longarm said, "Hey, Chico. You coming to knock on my door? What for?"

The young man said, "Mr. Long, there is a lady here to see you. She waits in the lobby."

Longarm furrowed his brow. "A lady? To see me?"

"Yes, a very pretty lady." The boy was about fifteen years old, so consequently he put a great deal of emphasis on the word "pretty."

Longarm thought. In the week that he had been in Taos, he hadn't met any women who would come calling on him. He asked, "Are you sure that you have the right man, Chico?"

The boy nodded vigorously. "She asked for the Marshal Custis Long. The United States Marshal Custis Long."

Custis frowned. "Nobody is supposed to know that I am a deputy marshal, Chico. I explained that to you when you saw the badge. They might try to put me to work. Let's be trying to keep that to ourselves."

Chico said, "I didn't tell the lady, Marshal Long. She asked for you like that. I don't know how she know you're a marshal. I don't know how she know you're here, but she came in asking for you. She is dressed very nice."

Longarm got up. "Well, go tell her that I will be right there. It beats the hell out of me who it could be. Did she give a name?"

As if it had suddenly came to him, Chico said, "Oh, yes. She is a Missus Baxter. A Missus Lily Gail Baxter."

Longarm almost staggered at the name. The last time he had seen her, her last name hadn't been Baxter. She had claimed that it was Wharton, but it could have been anything. He doubted that it was Baxter this time, if it was the same Lily Gail, and if was the same, he wasn't sure he wanted to see her. But if it was the same, maybe he *did* want to see her. If there was ever a woman who could create mixed emotions in him, it was Lily Gail.

Longarm said, "Chico, give me about five minutes and then bring her on back."

Chico asked, "You going to have her here in your room?"

Longarm smiled. He liked that choice of words. "Yes, Chico. I just might have her here in my room. You *comprende?* Run and tell her."

"Okay."

Longarm busied himself putting on a clean shirt and new socks, pulling on his boots, and brushing his hair. He had shaved that morning and he'd had a bath recently, so he was in pretty presentable shape.

As he prepared to wait for her arrival, he let his mind run back over his memories of Lily Gail, if indeed it was the same one—although it would be a strange coincidence if there was another Lily Gail. It had been over a year since he had seen her. She was without a doubt the most luscious piece of goods that he had ever encountered. She was about twenty-five or twenty-six, with startling blond hair that was like silk, and she was the very personification of sex as far as Longarm was concerned. A man seemed to melt into her while she seemed to envelop him. Longarm could still picture her erect breasts, which he always thought were about the size of a grapefruit,

6

although shaped different. They were topped with nipples like big red strawberries. He thought the most appealing thing about her was that she didn't know how desirable she was. Just thinking about her made his jeans get tight around the crotch.

The last time he had seen her, she had almost gotten him killed. She'd been attached to a gang that had been terrorizing Arkansas, Oklahoma, and parts of Texas and Kansas for several years. At the center of the gang had been three brothers, Rufus, Clem, and Vern Gallagher. Almost a year had passed from the time Lily Gail had successfully lured him into a trap. He had managed to extricate himself with the help of a couple of dozen cases of dynamite. In his escape, he had killed Vern Gallagher and had scattered the gang for a while. But Longarm, as well as every other lawman, knew that Rufus and Clem and their cousins and half cousins and friends were still very much in business.

He supposed he hated the Gallaghers about as much as any other outlaws he had ever come in contact with. They were murderers, they were rapists. For him they were a personal crusade, seeing that there was nothing that they wouldn't stoop to. They seemed to have no morals, no principles, no stopping place. If cruelty, if viciousness, if mere brutality was called for, then the Gallaghers were your men. Their trademark was leaving no witnesses and their hallmark was fire. If they robbed a ranch of cattle and horses, they would burn the ranch house and all of the buildings. If they robbed a bank, they would set it on fire along with half of the town it was in. They would even burn the wagons of the stores they looted or the armed vehicles carrying bullion that they stole from the gold mines. Dynamite was another one of their trademarks. What they couldn't burn, they blew up. For Longarm, the

7

Gallaghers were personal, very personal.

What made them so difficult to catch was that they had friends and relations all over the several regions they operated in. As soon as they pulled a raid, they would simply melt into the general populace. The man who, the day before, had been involved in blowing up a bank and killing a half-dozen innocent people could be found the next day working cattle, or cutting hay, or shoveling manure, looking for all the world like an honest farmer or rancher. No one would turn the Gallaghers in. Part of that was because of their relations with the country folks in the area, who thought they were some sort of heroes because they would disperse a little of their ill-gotten gains among some of the poorer people. The main reason it was difficult to get information about them was that the Gallaghers had a way of finding out who it was who'd talked and then taking their retaliation.

They were a frightening bunch.

And Lily Gail was no less frightening. The thing about her was that she had the innocent primness of a young lady Sunday School teacher and the wanton lust of the most insatiable nymphomaniac. She always acted the innocent. He knew she was about as innocent as a rattlesnake. She had kept Longarm chained in a barn for four days while waiting for the Gallaghers to come and kill him, and in the meantime had teased him with views of her naked body. In the end, it had been her own overpowering lust that had allowed him to escape.

And now, perhaps, here she was again. Lily Gail Baxter this time. The last time, she had claimed to be married to a half cousin of the Gallaghers, a man named Wharton. Well, he thought, perhaps she had married another half cousin. But the thing that you wanted to remember about Lily Gail, he reminded himself, was that you didn't want to believe a single word of what she said and less than half of what you saw her do.

But he could not keep himself from feeling excited at the prospect of burying and burrowing into that white, soft, luscious body again.

At that moment there came another knock on the door. Longarm crossed to it swiftly and flung it open. It was Chico again. He asked, "Where the hell is she, Chico?"

Chico said, "The lady say it no proper to come to your room. She say you have to come to the lobby. Marshal, I think the very pretty lady is right."

Longarm swore softly. "Very proper indeed. This must be a different Lily Gail."

"What do you want me to tell her, Marshal Long?"

"Quit calling me Marshal, Chico. Go on back there and tell her that I will be out in a couple of minutes. Tell me this, is she blond and real pretty?"

Chico grinned and rolled his eyes. "She plenty pretty, Marshal Long. Yes, she is blond."

"Well, go ahead and tell her that I will be there in just a moment." Longarm shut the door.

He sat on the bed, poured himself out some whiskey, and lit a small cigar. He knew Lily Gail hadn't hunted him up, however she had done it, just to see how excited she could get him. She'd come from the Gallaghers, sure as hell. If she had, he wondered what he was going to do about it. There was, after all, his vacation to think about, and secondly, he was not about to allow her to lure him into another trap of any kind, luscious body or not.

With his mind firmly fixed that there was no way that she could tempt him, he finally finished the whiskey in his glass, snubbed out his cigar, put on his hat, and went out to the lobby. He spotted her immediately; it was impossible not to. Not because the lobby was so small, but by her

9

striking head of golden blond hair and the wonderfully innocent little-girl face and wonderfully seductive big girl's body. She was sitting on a small settee against the far wall near the desk where guests registered.

Longarm walked across the tiled floor, his spurs going *ching-ching-ching* as he walked. She delayed looking at him until he was almost to her, and then, in what he took to be almost a practiced gesture, she jerked her head up to stare into his eyes, put her hand up to her mouth, and said, "Oh, you startled me, Marshal Long."

He took off his hat and sat down beside her, laughing. He said, "Lily Gail, the last time anybody startled you was when they quit before you wanted them to. How have you been?"

She gave him one of her innocent looks. "Why, Marshal, I have been just fine, in spite of the fact that someone, who will go nameless, blew up my ranch house and my barn and killed half of my cattle and my hired hands."

He threw back his head and laughed out loud. Lily Gail confused him. He couldn't determine if she was smartly dumb or dumbly smart. He knew she was an awful lot smarter than she acted, but he wasn't sure if she wasn't also as dumb as she acted. He said, "If you will forgive me, Lily Gail, that's not quite the way I remember it. As well as I can recall, I was chained to a post in your barn for several days, and the only relief I had from the boredom was the prospect of the Gallaghers coming to tear me apart between two horses and the occasional glimpse of you by moonlight."

She blushed prettily. She said, giving him a slap on the thigh, "Why, Marshal Long, you're not a gentleman to refer to that."

"What? Me being torn apart by horses or me getting an occasional glimpse of you?"

Lily Gail gave him a shy smile. "You old silly. You know what I mean."

Longarm said, "Well, before we go to swapping lies here, how about you telling me how you found me here, Lily Gail? I'm on leave of absence right now. I'm not even working. I'm just drinking whiskey and playing cards and having a rest. How in the hell did you get on to me?"

"Well, maybe I told a little lie," she said with a sly smile.

"That would be the first one, correct?"

"Now, Marshal, you shouldn't tease me."

"Well, all right. What kind of a little lie did you tell?"

"I sort of sent a telegram to your office in Denver, Colorado. I remember many times you telling me that was your headquarters. I said that you were desperately needed on family business and asked where could you be reached."

"And they wired you back and told you that I was in Taos?"

"Yes, at the Grand Hotel."

He looked off in the distance. "When I get back, there's going to be one less clerk in the U.S. marshals service."

"Oh, you mustn't mind. Otherwise, I wouldn't have had this chance to see you."

Longarm said, "How come you wouldn't come back to my room, Lily Gail?"

She gave him an amazed look. "Well, what kind of girl do you think I am, Marshal? Go to a gentleman's room? In the middle of the day?"

"Oh, I might have known. Of course. The middle of the day. That makes sense to me, too. If it had been night, that would have been different."

She said, "Well, I certainly am not going to answer that, but it certainly would have seemed more seemly. But to

11

visit a gentleman's room in the middle of the afternoon like I was coming to bring his laundry or something . . ."

Longarm shook his head. "Lily Gail, you beat anything I have even seen in my life. What are you doing these days? Are you still working for the Gallaghers?"

She said, "Marshal Long, I resent you saying such a thing about me. The Gallaghers are outlaws. They're misunderstood, and yet they are still considered outlaws. I resent you accusing me of having a formal association with them. The very idea!"

He gave her a frank look. "Are you here because of the Gallaghers?"

"As it happens, I do have a message to you from them."

Longarm said, "I wonder why that doesn't surprise me, Lily Gail. And by the way, where did you get the new name Baxter? Did you make that up?"

She folded her arms. "I'll have you know, that's my married name."

"So you got married again. Who did you marry this time?"

"A Mister Baxter. A Mister Jonas Baxter. A gentleman in trade back in Enid, Oklahoma."

"What kind of trade? Does he sell dynamite to the Gallaghers?"

"He was in the haberdashery trade, if you must know."

"Where is Mister Baxter?"

She cast her eyes down. "Unfortunately, Mister Baxter is no longer with us. He met an untimely end."

Longarm laughed. "Being married to you is about like being married to a black widow spider. Your husbands don't seem to last very long, Lily Gail. And I can testify that being one of your lovers ain't all that much safer."

Lily Gail said, "Oh, you've grown cold, Custis Long. You've grown cold and hard."

Longarm had to laugh again. "You hang around with the worse bunch of cutthroats and murderers and backshooting sonofabitches that this part of the country has ever seen and you call me cold?"

She said, "Longarm, that's what I'm here to talk to you about. You know, the Gallagher brothers have been done a terrible injustice. They are misunderstood. They've been prosecuted and persecuted by the law and it hasn't been fair. You even killed poor Vern, and he meant you nothing but the best."

Longarm said, "Wait a minute. Let's get the record straight, Lily Gail, before you go off on another one of your dreams while you are still awake. Now, the way it was, you lured me out to your ranch north of Wichita Falls, Texas, and then you doped me by putting laudanum in my whiskey. After I had passed out, your hired hand or your lover, whoever he was, chained me out in the barn before he went off to get the Gallaghers, who had every intention of killing me. The fact is that I happened to get loose and set that dynamite off, in which explosion Vern Gallagher got killed. Now, do not represent the Gallaghers to me as anything but what they really are. By the way, where are you staying?"

She said primly, "I have just a short while ago come into town. I have not as of yet taken accommodations. My mission has been to deliver this invitation to you from the two remaining Gallagher brothers."

Longarm gave her a guarded look. "And just what would that invitation be?"

"They want to meet with you. They want to try to put an end to this terrible persecution that the law has seen fit to visit upon them. They think that perhaps ya'll can make some kind of a deal. They admit that, from time to time, they have had some terrible people working for them and that they have done some terrible things, and they are willing to surrender these people to the law if ya'll would just give them a good letting alone."

Longarm burst out laughing. He couldn't help himself. He said, "You mean, they've found some poor saps that they are going to turn in so as to save their own skins? Isn't that about the size of it? Where are the Gallaghers right now?"

"They are camped on the Cimarron Strip, not even seventy miles from here."

Longarm knew she was talking about that part of Oklahoma that bled off at the top of the territory like a string of spilt milk, running across the panhandle of Texas and below western Kansas and eastern Colorado, ending at the New Mexico border.

For a second, it shocked him to realize they were so close. He looked quickly around the hotel lobby to see if there might be any strangers who could be allowing Lily Gail to lead them to him, but the lobby was mostly deserted except for a few familiar faces. Nevertheless, Longarm said, "I don't much care to be sitting out here in the open with you, Lily Gail, with the Gallaghers anywhere near."

"You don't have to worry about that. They have sent me in to see if I couldn't persuade you to take a trip over the line to meet with them and see if something couldn't be worked out."

Longarm looked at her with amazement. "Lily Gail, have you lost what little mind you ever had? I can't make any deals with the Gallaghers, even if I wanted to, which I damn sure don't. The only way I would meet with them is if I had a troop of calvary behind me. The Gallaghers could raise half a hundred men at a moment's notice. If you think that you're going to lead me into some trap out in the flatlands of the Cimarron Strip, you've got another think coming, girl. I mean, you are a pleasure in bed, but you ain't worth dying for."

She gave a pouty look and gazed up at him with that innocent lewdness in her eyes, the look that, if a whore could copy, would be worth a million dollars to her. She said, "The last time I saw you, you said you hadn't had all of me that you wanted, just all that you could take." She put her hand on his thigh, still gazing up at him. "Do you still mean that?" As she said it, she leaned slightly forward, thrusting her breasts at him.

He looked her over carefully. For a change, she was wearing a yellow print frock that was closed at the neck with a lace collar. It had balloon sleeves and a tight-fitting waist and bodice and then ran snugly down over her hips. He could see that it was an expensive garment, and he could see that she was wearing patent-leather slippers. He supposed the Gallaghers had been good to her of late, or she had found someone else with very loose scruples.

Longarm said, "Like I said, I don't like being out here talking about the Gallaghers. Why don't we go on back to my room and discuss this matter?"

She said, "Oh, no. I couldn't do that." She smoothed the material of her dress in her lap with her chubby little white hands. "That wouldn't be right, for a lady to go to a gentleman's bedroom in the middle of the day."

Longarm pulled out his watch. "Lily Gail, it is going on half past four. That's nearly the shank of the evening. It wouldn't be as if you were going in there right after lunch."

She looked thoughtful, and then looked up at him with that same innocent look. "Did you know that I am not wearing a thing on underneath this dress? Can you imagine? This morning, when I got dressed, I forgot all about my underclothes."

15

Longarm could suddenly feel the pulse beating in his ears. He said, "Is that a fact?"

She nodded slowly. "Of course, with the weather being so unseasonably warm, it is more comfortable this way."

"Well, you probably have had a long trip. I think we should go back and let you rest. Perhaps I could order you a bath."

She smiled with her cupid-bow mouth, her red full lips. "Now, that would be proper, wouldn't it?"

He nodded vigorously. "Oh, yes. That would be more than proper."

She smiled again. "Well, so as not to give anyone the wrong idea, for certainly we wouldn't be doing anything wrong, why don't you walk along ahead of me and I will follow you?"

He stood up. "All right, Lily Gail, but just make sure that you don't pick up any company on the way back. It's on this floor, the fourth door on the left, down the hall in that direction." He nodded his head across the lobby.

"I don't know what you mean by not bringing any company. I am simply trying to keep up proper appearances, as Mister Baxter would have said."

"I've noticed that you are talking a great deal more high-toned here of late, although I'm not sure that you know all the words that you are saying. Did you get that from the late Mister Baxter?"

She nodded gravely and said, "He was a very well-educated man. In trade, you know. Haberdashery. Gentlemen's clothing. A very high-toned establishment."

Longarm said, "I'm on my way. I'll expect you in about two minutes."

She nodded. "That will be agreeable with me."

Chapter 2

It was a few minutes more than a couple of minutes when he heard the tiny knock at the door. He opened it with his revolver in his hand, but it was just Lily Gail. He let her in, closed the door carefully, and then turned the key in the lock. He had windows on two sides, one on the side street and one toward the alley, but he'd carefully pulled the shades down so that no outsiders could see in.

He said, "Why don't we sit down and have a drink? I don't have any lemonade, which I know that you like, but I'll water down your whiskey so that it's not so strong."

She unbuttoned the collar of her dress and then the next button and then the next, so that he could begin to see the cleavage of her breasts. She said, "That would be ever so nice. You will be pleased to learn that, with Mister Baxter, I learned to enjoy an occasional drink of whiskey. Mister Baxter approved of it and said that it seemed to make me even more lively."

"The prospect of you being any more lively in bed is frightening."

She said, "Why, Mister Custis Long. I'm not sure that's a proper remark to make to a lady."

He laughed. "Lily Gail, in spite of everything, I'm glad to see you. I know that you're here for a purpose that's not going to do me a bit of good if you have your way, but I'm glad to see you."

As Lily Gail accepted the glass of whiskey from his hand, she said, "It's just some little old piddling thing that the Gallagher brothers asked if I would do. They know that you and I are acquainted and that you would be inclined to trust me."

That caused Longarm to throw back his head and laugh out loud again. If there was anybody that he was not going to trust, ever again, it was Lily Gail, even if he got what he wanted from her. He realized that there were some folks who might think that such calculations were not of a gentlemanly nature, but they didn't know Lily Gail as well as he knew her.

She was sitting a few feet away from him in a straight-backed chair. Longarm was sitting on the side of the bed, handy to the whiskey. He held his glass up and said, "Let's drink to old times, Lily Gail. Here's a toast for you. Bottoms up."

She giggled and took a good healthy swig of her whiskey and water. He followed suit, keeping his eye on her. He said, "Lily Gail, that next button is looking mighty loose. It looks like you're throwing a strain on it. You might want to undo it so as to save the thread."

She said, "Oh," and looked down quickly. "If I am losing another button . . ." She stopped and gave him a look. "Why, Mister Custis Long, you're trying to trick me into unbuttoning my dress."

"Yeah, there's that old devil in me, Lily Gail. I don't know what makes me get up to such things."

18

With that innocent, guileless look on her face, she unbuttoned the button, and the strain of her breasts pushed the material of her dress back enough so that the V widened and he could see the rise of those milky white breasts. He could see the side of one of the big pink rosettes that made the nests for her big nipples.

He said, "Drink your drink, Lily Gail, and let me fix you another." As an encouragement he downed his and then poured more whiskey in his glass. She followed him, quickly finishing hers, and leaned forward to hand him her glass. As she did, he could see clearly down the front of her dress. "My, my, Lily Gail, I do believe they have grown," he said. "They're two of the prettiest puppies that I have ever seen."

She blushed prettily and made a feeble attempt at holding her dress together. "If you are not the beatingest, Longarm. You don't care how you talk to a girl."

He said, "Stand up, Lily Gail, I want to see something."

She stood up. "What?"

Longarm said, "Lift your skirt."

She automatically took hold of her skirt and lifted it to her knees.

He said, "Higher."

"Why, Mister Long, how forward of you." She slowly lifted it until the hem came creeping up her thighs to reveal that golden patch of flaxen hair that topped the soft little mound at the vee of her creamy thighs. That golden triangle, if anything, was more burnished than her hair. He'd had his face there before and he intended, if things went right, to have it there again before the day was out. Still staring at her, he set his glass down on the bedside table and stood up, unbuckling his gunbelt as he did. He let it fall to the floor.

19

Longarm started toward her. As he did, she dropped the skirt of her dress and began unbuttoning the rest of her buttons. By the time he reached her, she had them undone down past her waist. He took her dress by the shoulders and pushed it gently off her so that it fell softly to the floor. As he did, her arms came up around his neck and she drew his mouth down to hers. Her lips were full and ripe and her tongue was a probing, caressing, darting messenger of passion. He could feel her hands go inside between his and begin to unbutton his shirt. He had his arms around her waist, and he held her tightly to him as he walked backwards slowly toward the bed. When he felt the bed against the back of his legs, he started to fall over backwards, but she held him up. Lily Gail finished unbuttoning his shirt and then tore it off his shoulders. She dropped to her knees and unbuckled his pants and dropped them around his ankles. With both hands, she guided his member into her mouth. He let out a long rising sigh as he went inside her, and he grabbed the back of her head as she began to pump back and forth on him. He said, his voice faint, "Oh, heavens, Lily Gail, you'd better stop. You'd better not do that."

She put her arms around him and held herself tightly in place while she kept her head moving. He stood it as long as he could, and then forcibly lifted her to her feet. Her mouth went straight to his and stayed there as they fell over backwards on the bed. Her dress had stayed where it had fallen on the floor, but he was still encumbered by his boots and his jeans. He rolled her off for an instant and reached down to kick his boots off, but he only got one off and one pants leg free before she pulled him back to her.

She was shivering in excitement next to him, panting, her breaths coming in short gasps, her mouth busy over

20

his face and neck. He tried to roll over on top of her, his mouth seeking the nipple of her breast, but she pushed him back and got on top of him. In his ear she said breathily, "This is ladies' choice."

Her lips and tongue against his ear made little shivers run all through his body. Before he realized what was happening, she had taken him inside her, sinking him deeper and deeper into her. She was over him, her breasts at the level of his chin. He moved his face to envelop one of the big red strawberry-tipped milk-white orbs.

Over him, she was gasping and sighing, her fingers gripping his shoulders as she rotated and rose and fell against him. He put his arms around her, drawing her down to him, feeling her softness almost melt into him. It went on and on until he felt like he was climbing a stairway that kept getting steeper and steeper.

She suddenly let out a long, shuddering cry, and at that instant he exploded, thrusting sharply up against her. She kept screaming, her head down, the sound muffled by his neck. They were fused, holding each other tightly by their arms.

How long it lasted, he didn't know. All he knew was that he had somehow reached the top of that long, steep stair and then had fallen off the other end. It had been a long tumble, but now he lay on the ground, gasping for breath, spent by the long climb and then the fall. The breath had been knocked out of him by the landing. She slowly slid off his side, her mouth open, gasping for air.

After a period of time had passed, he slowly sat up on the side of the bed. He was amazed to see that he was still in the hotel room, that they were still on the bed, that Lily Gail was still lying crosswise, and that he still had on one boot and his jeans down around his ankles. He was amazed to see the whiskey in the glasses. He felt like a

21

man who had just traveled halfway around the world. He didn't expect to arrive back at the same place, not after such a trip.

When he could, he said, "Wow, Lily Gail. I've been on some rides before, but I believe that was the best one that I've ever taken. Look at this . . . my hands are shaking."

When she didn't answer, he glanced around at her. She was lying there, her beautiful body in perfect repose with her eyes closed. Nothing could have excited him at that instant. He was drained, spent, finished, but yet even in that condition, he had to admire the perfection of her female body. He didn't know if she was asleep or not, and he didn't much care right then. What he wanted was a drink and a smoke and a short rest.

As best as he could, he pulled his jeans up and put his other boot on. Then he reached over and drank the glass of whiskey that he had poured out but had never finished once Lily Gail had lifted her skirt. Her drink was there also and he drank that, in spite of the fact that it had been watered. After that, he felt better. He found a small cigarillo and then lit it, blowing out a cloud of smoke and shaking his head. "I've got to admit, Lily Gail, that I had forgotten. I've been with many women, but you've got to be the best. I don't know what it is that you do. I don't know how it is that you do it, but you can suck a man dry better than any woman I have ever had. That thing of yours seems to open up and suck a man right on in there. It's amazing. It's like you have little fingers in there."

He looked around at her again. She was still lying silently with her eyes closed, but he could see that her breathing was smoothing out. He thought she would be all right in a moment. He became aware of his neck hurting slightly, and put his hand up and felt the left side. It was moist.

He pulled his hand away and looked and saw that it was bleeding.

He said, "Why, you little bitch. You bit me, dammit."

He crossed the room to the basin stand. There was a mirror on the wall and he could clearly see the outline of her teeth in his neck. He hadn't felt a thing, such had been his passion. He said, "Well, damn you, Lily Gail. I ought to take a razor strap to your rear end for that little stunt. If I thought you had done it on purpose, I would."

He crossed back to the whiskey bottle, poured some on a little towel, and placed it to the bite. It burned like hell and made him say damn several times until the burning subsided. Then he swabbed it off lightly until it finally stopped bleeding. It really wasn't a very bad cut. He had been bitten by a woman before, but he was amazed that he hadn't been aware of it when it happened.

He fixed two more drinks, one watered, and then sat down on the bed. He turned to the left and then set hers on her slightly rounded stomach. "Here's a drink," he said. "Maybe you'll take this instead of sucking the blood out of me. I've never heard of such a thing."

Her lips came up into a little smile, and she reached her hands up and clutched the glass with both hands. She still hadn't opened her eyes. She said softly, "Oh, my, Mister Custis Long. That was ever so nice. Are you so nice to all of your girlfriends?"

He said dryly, "Lily Gail, I wouldn't exactly classify you as a girlfriend." He took another drink of whiskey and began pulling on the rest of his clothes. When he had his jeans buttoned and belted, he reached down and picked up Lily Gail's dress from where it lay on the floor and carried it over and draped it over the back of a chair that was against the wall. He noticed how crisp and fresh it was. He looked back over his shoulder and said, "Lily

Gail, did you tell me that you weren't staying anyplace in Taos, that you had just gotten here?"

"That's right."

"And I'm to believe that you came from seventy miles out on the Cimarron Strip where it is hot enough to fry an egg on a rock right now and that you arrived in this freshly starched and ironed dress with your hair all done up perfect and all that rouge on your face and not a drop of sweat on you? Do you really want me to believe that?"

She looked at him round-eyed. "Why, whatever do you mean?"

He laughed. "Girl, I may have been born yesterday, but I wasn't born the day before. Now, where are you staying? You walked into this hotel from someplace else where you got yourself all gussied up, and it damned sure wasn't someplace out on the strip."

She said, trying to sound indignant but not succeeding, "Why, Mister Long. That is certainly no way to talk to a lady. I have not misled you, as you seem to think. Did I once say that I had come from the strip? I said the Gallaghers had been on the strip, but I never once said that I was out there."

Longarm gave her a long look. "You said you had just come from the Gallaghers and they were on the Cimarron Strip."

"I said the Gallagher brothers want to meet you on the strip because they are comfortable in Oklahoma Territory."

Longarm said, "I'm well aware of that, Lily Gail. Since they have bought off every sheriff in the territory, I can well understand why. Do you mean they are not on the strip right now? Where are they? Right here in town? I wouldn't be at all surprised that you've led them to me and that they're about to burst through the door at any moment."

She said, "How you talk. There you go again. Such thoughts should never enter your mind. I arrived here from Raton, New Mexico, this morning, Mister Long, as if it is any of your business. I arrived here by train and I came straight to this hotel."

Longarm looked at her again while he casually poured himself another drink. He said, "Let me get this straight. The Gallaghers want to meet me on the strip to turn over a bunch of small-fry in return for some kind of pardon for them. Is that what they are talking about?"

She fluttered her hands above her naked body. "I don't know about that sort of thing. All I know is that they want to talk to you and they want to surrender some hooligans who have been doing some bad things in their name. All they want is a chance to have a talk with you and show you that they ain't near as bad as they've been made out to be."

Longarm laughed. "Nobody could make the Gallaghers out to be any worse than they already are." He leaned down, took the edge of the bedspread, and flipped it across the bed. "Here, cover yourself with this while I think. You're too much of a distraction for a man to get any serious thinking in when you're lying there like that."

"Well, pardon me!"

"Lily Gail, just be quiet for a moment." He took a straight-backed chair, set it in front of the window that faced the side street, raised the shade, and then sat there with a glass of whiskey in his hand and a small cigar in his mouth, staring out thoughtfully while his mind considered all of the possibilities. Of course he was interested in any meeting, any confrontation with the Gallaghers. They were so elusive, so nigh on to invisible, that to even catch scent of them, much less sight, not to mention the sight over a gun barrel, even at considerable risk was worth the

25

chance. He had no intention of buying into the game as they had it set up. He was no more going to ride out alone to meet the Gallaghers on the broad flat plains of western Oklahoma than he was going to join the Women's Christian Temperance Union. He sat thinking, reviewing his options. He could wire Denver for some more deputies for assistance, but he was against that idea for two reasons. First, it might turn out to be nothing but a hoax and he hated to pull other marshals off their jobs to come up with nothing. Second, he'd told Billy Vail that he was on leave, that if Billy Vail bothered him with anything even remotely resembling law work, he would not only burn Billy Vail's house and barn down, he would burn his neighbor's house and barn down so that he would no longer be such a popular man. In short, he didn't want to give Billy Vail any more ammunition than he already had to needle him with, and if he instigated some law work on his own, Billy Vail would cackle like the old hen he was.

Longarm took another drink of whiskey and continued to watch the slow traffic in the street. Unfortunately, he didn't know any of the law around Taos, not well enough to risk his life with them. The only man he could think of who was in town or nearby was an old friend of some twenty years standing. Fisher Lee had been a sheriff down in south Texas until he had given up the job because of what he considered an ungrateful public who really didn't want law and order. Now he was a professional gambler. Fish was a steady hand in a fight and a good man in almost any circumstance. More important, Longarm knew he could count on Fish's help and he knew where he could lay his hands on him within the hour.

Longarm said, "When am I supposed to give you an answer?"

She said primly, "My train returns to Raton this evening by six. I'm supposed to bring an answer back by then."

He said, "Hell, that don't leave much time, Lily Gail. You ought to be up and dressing. I don't think I can give you an answer by then."

She said, "Well, I can take the train in the morning then and spend the night. That's what I was told."

He gave her a slow smile. "Lily Gail, I don't know if you are aware of it or not, but I can arrest you right here on the spot. You're in the employ of wanted felons, which makes you an accessory to everything from cattle theft to murder. I could throw you in prison for ten years."

She gave him a round-mouth look. "Oh, now you wouldn't do that, now would you, Custis?"

He chuckled. "Oh, well, not before in the morning, anyway."

Longarm got up and walked over and refilled his glass. "Did the Gallaghers say how many of these two-bit small-fry they were going to surrender?"

"Well, not in round numbers, but I think it's somewhere around a dozen."

Longarm laughed and shook his head. "Well, that must have been some bargain. I guess the Gallaghers gave them a choice: either be slow-roasted over a fire or pull a little prison time. I guess it wasn't too hard a decision to come to."

Lily Gail said anxiously, "Oh, no, that's not the way of it at all, Custis. The Gallaghers, they captured these men and they have them ready to turn over to you."

Longarm said, "Lily Gail, you're good at one thing, why don't you just stick to that."

She tossed her head. "That's an awful mean thing to say, Custis. Do you realize the last time we were together you got my hair all muddy in that old barn."

27

He stared at her in amazement. What she was talking about was the struggle to get the keys to unlock himself from the chains that had bound him to the center post of the barn where he was being held. His struggle had been made more desperate because he knew the Gallaghers were only a few hours away and that his life was hanging in the balance. Now she was talking about him getting her hair muddy. Well, that was Lily Gail for you, he thought.

Longarm said in a sincere-sounding voice, "Lily Gail, you know, I've lain awake nights thinking about what I did to your hair. I can't tell you the amount of sleep that I've lost over that."

For a second, she almost smiled. Then she wrinkled her brow in thought before slapping the mattress with the flat of her hand. She said, "Oh, you're just saying that. You're not sorry at all."

Longarm shook his head slowly. "Ain't nothing gets by you, is there, Lily Gail. You're too hard a nut to crack for me, I'll tell you." Then his tone of voice changed. He said briskly, "You had better get up and get dressed. We need to eat some supper here before too long. Obviously, you won't be going back to Raton tonight, since I can't make up my mind what I want to do by the time the evening train leaves."

She said, "You just think you're going to have your lustful way with me, don't you, Mister Deputy Marshal Custis Long? I know how you think and that's the reason you're going to make me stay over, now isn't it?"

He grinned at her. "I'll make you a deal, Lily Gail. I'll leave you alone if you'll leave me alone. Now, how's that?"

"Ha! You don't mean that!"

"Try me."

"You sound like you don't like me anymore."

"Like you? Lily Gail, you're about as likable as rotgut whiskey. Drink that, and you don't realize the damage you're doing to yourself until it's too late."

"I guess that's not supposed to be a compliment, is it?"

"Lily Gail, just study on it. Now, get up and get dressed. I've got to do some hard thinking tonight and I've got to go and find a man."

"And what am I supposed to be doing while you're gadding about the town?"

"Well, if you want me to do what you've been sent to get me to do, then you'll stay right here in this room. I'd be happy if you walked on out and caught the train and I never saw you again. I'm willing to maybe go along with this idea that the Gallaghers have thought up, but I'm not in love with it. You make up your mind what you're going to do."

"Well, all right, if you're going to be like that about it, but you won't be out too late, will you?"

Longarm said, "We'll see."

Chapter 3

Longarm and Fisher Lee sat at a table in a corner of a low-ceilinged smoky saloon not far from Longarm's hotel. The saloon could have been one of fifty in the town, but for some reason it was a gathering place for real high-money poker players. Fisher Lee was there almost every night. Now, they sat talking over a couple of drinks. Longarm was drinking good Spanish brandy, but Fisher, because he would be playing most of the night, was contenting himself with a beer.

Fisher Lee was a man of about forty. He was tall and lean and seemed slow of movement and slow of reaction. Nothing could have been further from the truth. Longarm considered him as fine a man with a gun as he'd ever served with. Fisher's even temper and ready laugh had led more than one fool into making a mistake about him, either in a card game or a gunfight.

Longarm said, "So, what do you think, Fish? How does it look to you?" He had just finished telling his friend the details of the proposition Lily Gail had brought him.

Fisher put back his head and laughed good-humoredly. "What do I think, Longarm? I believe it's a trap or else somebody has gotten word to them that you've lost your mind."

Longarm nodded. "That's what's got me so puzzled about the whole damn thing. Do they really think I'm such a damn fool that I would ride out in the bald-ass prairie and be a target for those damn Gallaghers? I've killed one, but I'd like another, maybe two more."

Fisher Lee, who knew as much about the Gallaghers as anyone, although his law work had never brought him into contact with them, nodded. "Yeah, I heard about you blowing one of them out of the county with a stick of dynamite. It's too bad the whole damn bunch of them weren't with him."

Longarm said, "Well, what the hell do you suppose they are up to?"

Fisher shook his head. "I don't know. I can't figure it out. There is this, though, Longarm. You do have a certain reputation." Fisher cut his eyes sideways at the deputy marshal. "You may not be aware of it, but there are some folks who believe you're damn fool enough to try anything."

Longarm said, "Bullshit. Anyone that knows me knows that's not the case. I didn't get to stay alive this long by being a damn fool."

Fisher nodded. "I know that and you know that. I know that you won't walk through a door without knowing what is on the other side and who is backing you up. But lots of folks see you do things that they think are taking chances, though in fact you've planned out every detail and you ain't really taking a chance. The other fellow is taking the chance but he doesn't know it. The Gallaghers figure that you want a piece of their ass so bad that you'd risk a dumb play like that. That you would take that kind of a chance, that you'd be so damned cocky that you would walk out there and try to tie their hands behind their backs."

Longarm took a sip of his drink. "Well, I never thought folks had that opinion of me. Is it widespread?"

Fisher said, "Well, I guess you'd say it was the folks kind of on the fringe of the action that think that way. Them that know you a little better have got a pretty good line on what you will and won't do."

Longarm got out his watch and looked at it. It was going on nearly ten o'clock. He knew that Fisher's game would be starting soon, and he wanted to get back to the hotel and check on Lily Gail, although at that point he wasn't too sure if he wouldn't have been as happy to see her disappear.

Fisher said, grinning at Longarm, "I kind of like the bait they sent in to try and reel you in. Sounds like a pretty tasty morsel to me."

Longarm grimaced. "That woman is more dangerous than a bear in a closet. Sometimes you'd think she's nearly sane, and then she'll think or do something that will convince you that she ain't got a lick of sense."

Fisher gave him a bemused look. "Ya'll talk alot, do ya?"

Longarm smiled slightly. "She's one of the best at that."

"Talking?"

"You know what I mean, Fish. Listen . . ." He paused. "Would you be available to help me on this matter if I can ever sit down and think of some kind of a plan?"

Fisher sat back in his chair and said slowly, "I'd like to have a look at your hand before I make a decision on a question like that, Longarm. We've been friends for a long time and I'd like to see us continue being friends for a long time, but that might turn out to be difficult if one of us is dead."

33

Longarm said, "I'm not planning on that direction, but I'll tell you, Fish, a clean shot at those Gallaghers is just damn near more than I can resist. I've been trying to bring them bastards to book for five, six, hell, maybe even seven years, and all I've been able to do is kill ten or twelve of their hired hands and one of the brothers. Sonofabitch, would I like to get my hands on that bunch."

Fisher said, "That kind of talk makes me nervous, Longarm. You're getting the bit in your teeth now. You're starting to talk like a runaway."

"Yeah, that sort of does sound like dumb talk, doesn't it? Don't worry, Fish, I won't get you off in a storm. I just need to know if I can count on you for some light work if I can get a handle on this situation."

Fisher looked at his beer for a moment and then drank off half of it. "Well, if the odds are no worse than five to two, then yeah, I reckon you could count me in, but try and narrow it down if you can."

"I've got to find out what this is all about first, but I don't even know how to go about doing that."

Fisher gave Longarm a shrewd look. "It's my belief that wherever that Miss Lily Gail came from is where your Gallagher brothers are right now. I don't think they're camped out on the Cimarron Strip. They don't strike me as the kind to lead the harsh life, not with the kind of money they have. I reckon that wherever she came from, that's where they are sitting, waiting for the answer. Now, you're supposed to meet them just over the line in Oklahoma Territory. Well, they can be there in a day's ride if they came from Raton. In fact, they can be there before you can be there from here."

Longarm thought for a moment. "Then maybe I might need somebody to follow Miss Lily Gail back to where she came from that she don't know."

Fisher gave him an eye. "You're talking about taking up a considerable amount of my time, Longarm, running around chasing that female of yours. Do you know how much I can make in here a night playing poker with some of these big-monied ranchers that have more money than they have sense?"

Longarm said, "No, but I know how much you can lose when you get cold. How's your luck been running here lately, Fish?"

"Now, Longarm, you know luck ain't got nothing to do with poker playing."

Longarm gave him a slim smile. "I'm not really sure that you've learned that yet, Fish. You're still kind of a streak player. Sometimes you're hot and it's fine, but I've seen you get cold and still bet against your luck."

Fisher laughed. "You're never going to let me forget those few times that you've bested me at a poker table, are you? I hate to disappoint you, Longarm, but I play different than I used to. I play now for the money. I believe those people at the table have what is rightfully mine and they've held it long enough."

Longarm nodded. "I've heard those words from men who dress a lot nicer than you do, Fish, although I have to admit, you're looking mighty dapper tonight. Where did you get that shiny leather vest? And that's a pretty fair pair of boots that you're wearing there. Also, that would appear to be a diamond ring on your finger. How is it that's not in a pawnshop?"

Fisher said, "Same old Longarm. Don't hurt yourself giving me too much credit now. You don't want to reach in your pocket and count money with me, do you, and see who has the most? The one with the most takes the other one's pile?"

Longarm grinned. "You wouldn't be trying to set me up for a sucker bet, now would you, Fisher?"

Before his friend could answer, three men came into the saloon, walked past them, and went to a table in the corner where two other men were sitting with a deck of cards, waiting. The men began pulling out rolls of bills, stacking them on the table in front of them. Longarm nodded his head their way and asked, "Is that your game?"

Fish pulled a face. "Not that bunch. That's a bunch of gut-cinch players. They don't bet unless they're damn certain they have the winning hand. You can sit there half the night buying the ante, and then all of a sudden you'll run into a full house or worse and get your brains beat out. I don't play in that game. Mine don't generally crank up until around eleven. We've got some pretty stiff players and we attract a few that aspire to play with the big boys, and we're only too willing to let them do so. But getting back to your problem. I might be willing to help you out on this matter, considering the fact that you haven't mentioned that you've saved my bacon on a couple of occasions. I'm surprised at you, Longarm. Are you losing your touch?"

Longarm smiled his thin smile. "I thought it would be more effective to let you remind yourself of it."

Fish said, "So you think it would be a good idea for me to follow that lady back to Raton and see who she meets there?"

"That might be a good way to start this business."

Fisher Lee got out a cigarette and lit it. "One thing we might be overlooking here, Longarm. I've never laid eyes on any one of the Gallagher brothers. Now, there is Rufus and Clem left. Rufus is the oldest and Clem is the youngest and Vern, the one you killed, was the middle one. Is that right?"

"That's the way I get it."

"Well, I've never seen them. Have you?"

"Now that you mention it, I haven't. Not at close range, anyway. I've seen them over rifle sights but not in range. No, I've got to agree with you. If you were to put a gun to my head and cock it, I couldn't tell you what any of them look like."

Fisher said, "That whole damn bunch is so inbred that half of the cousins are their own uncles. Hell, how are you supposed to know who you're talking with?"

Longarm said, "Maybe they've got some sort of distinguishing marks about them so that we can tell who is who."

"How are you going to find that out?"

"Well, I thought I'd ask Miss Lily Gail Baxter, the widow of a well-to-do haberdasher."

"However you want to play it, Longarm. I'll give you all the help I can. To tell you the truth, I probably need a vacation away from the table. I ain't just been tearing them up here lately. Have you any general plans of how you might go about this business once we make certain who we are dealing with?"

Longarm pushed his hat back and scratched his head. "I've been thinking about that. What I calculated was that I would make them a proposition. One of the brothers comes in, stays with you, and I'll go out and see the other brother, and in case I don't make it back, we'll just propose to put a bullet in the ear of the brother that you've got."

Fisher gave him a look. "What if the brother you're meeting will be happy to be done with the brother that I'm sitting with? That ain't going to do you a hell of a lot of good out there if he don't care if the other brother makes it back or not."

Longarm frowned. "Hell, Fish. The chance to get up close to either one of those Gallagher brothers is just too damn good of an opportunity to pass up. I've got to take a chance on this. All I'm trying to do is cut down on the risk."

Fisher shook his head. "I'm with you all the way on this, partner. But I've got to tell you, you're playing the other man's game and he is setting the odds. You and me both know that ain't no gamble—that's a good way to lose."

Longarm stood up. "You still got a room above this joint?"

"Yeah, when I'm in the room, which ain't too damn often."

"I need some more information, that's what I'm hurting for right now. Let me talk to that silly girl again and see what more I can find out, but the more I think about it, the more I'm convinced that the only safe way is to have one of the brothers in here with you while I go talk to the other one. Maybe you're right, maybe they won't care that much what happens to the other one. It appears that I'm betting my life on it and that ain't real smart, but dammit, Fish."

"I know. It's just too good a chance to pass up. I've stayed in some hands where the pot got so big that I couldn't fold just because it was so big, and all I did was throw good money after bad money because I didn't have the winning hand. Just because the pot is big doesn't mean it's going to be yours. But I hear what you're saying and I'm willing to do what I can to help, even if it means following that damn girl into Raton tomorrow."

Longarm rubbed his jaw. "Yeah, but like you said, that might not do much good. Even if the Gallagher brothers are both in Raton, you don't know what they look like. I don't know what you'd do about it even if I could get you a good enough description. They're slick customers, you know that, Fish."

"Hell, yes. How many years have they been operating?"

"Six, seven, hell, I don't know. It just seems that the only thing that I've heard about in this part of the country is the damn Gallagher brothers. What they haven't done ain't worth doing. Listen, I'll check in with you by ten or eleven o'clock in the morning. Will you be awake by then?"

Fisher shrugged and pulled a face. "That depends. The way these players have been treating me, I might get in bed early tonight and be up having breakfast well before then. I'll arrange to be somewhere handy around ten o'clock, but if things go right I may still be sitting over there at that table." He nodded toward a table in the other corner. "They ought to be showing up pretty quick."

Longarm nodded. "All right, let me go see what I can get out of her. Of course, you know what it is going to cost me."

Fisher nodded with mock sympathy. "You'll just do anything in furtherance of the law, won't you, Longarm? Including using your body? You're a hell of a fellow. Has anybody ever told you that?"

Longarm pointed a finger at him. "Go to hell, Fish. I'll see you in the morning. Stand pat with two high pair. Keep them guessing. Adios."

Longarm went out of the saloon into the cool air of the New Mexico night. At that elevation, the air was crisp with a tinge of rain in it. Could be that they would get some relief from the heat of the days. But what he mainly needed relief from right now was Lily Gail's silliness. He didn't know how long it would take him to find out enough pertinent facts about the two remaining Gallagher brothers that would allow them to be identified. But then, any conversation with Lily Gail was a considerable chore.

As he walked back to his hotel, he went over and over in his mind any possibilities that he had overlooked. Fisher had wondered why he simply didn't bring in another federal marshal or two. He'd understood, however, when Longarm had explained his reasoning. And so far as the local law went, they wouldn't do him a bit of good in Oklahoma Territory, even if they wanted to go, which he seriously doubted that they would. Fisher had given his opinion that the local law wasn't to be trusted with anything more dangerous than taking a bribe. He'd said, "That's one of the reasons I've gotten out of the law business, Longarm. Maybe at your level it's all clean and nice and straight, but where I was, I never could depend on the man to my right, to my left, or behind me. The only person that I was sure of was the one in front of me and he was trying to kill me. Maybe had I gone the way you did, I'd feel different, but I have to tell you that being a local lawman in these territories, and even in some of the states, is the next thing to walking on quicksand. You never know where you are going to stand."

So in the end that brought it down to Longarm and the only man locally that he felt he could trust, Fisher Lee. What just the two of them could do against perhaps a dozen or two of the Gallaghers was anybody's guess. He knew Fisher was right, that he was drawing into a bad hand, one that he would ordinarily have folded. But to have them within reach was an itch that he just had to scratch. If you'd said that he was being brave or courageous, he'd have laughed in your face and called you a liar. In his mind, what he was doing was handling his job with the best judgment that he had at the time opportunity presented itself. Only time would tell if that judgment proved to be right or wrong. The pay was the same whether you were sitting behind a desk or running a risk of getting yourself killed. The government didn't particularly give a damn.

Longarm was somewhat surprised to find Lily Gail in his room when he opened the door and stepped inside. Even though the hour was late, knowing her, he'd halfway expected her to be looking helpless on the street or sitting in the lobby practicing that innocent flirtation that she was the innocent mistress of, but she was where he'd told her to be, surprising as it was. She was lying on the bed, completely naked. As he came in, she made a pretense of fanning herself with her hand. She said, "My, isn't it hot?"

Longarm crossed to the window that fronted the street and pulled the shade all the way down. The room was only dimly lit, but it was lit well enough for any interested passerby to have gotten a good glimpse of Lily Gail. He supposed that was her second favorite hobby, being viewed without any clothes on. For a moment he stood by the bed, gazing down at her. She was a wonder, all pink and white and golden. Even though he knew she was well into her twenties, she still seemed to have the remnants of baby fat in all the right places, and it made her seem even softer, on the sides of her breasts, in her chubby little hands and feet, and especially in the little mound where the golden silken hairs grew.

Longarm looked her over and said, "Lily Gail, you are shameless, did you know that?"

"Why, whatever do you mean, Mister Deputy Marshal Custis Long?"

He pulled up a chair and sat down by the bedside table with the whiskey and his cigars handy to reach. He poured himself half of a tumbler of the Maryland whiskey and then took a moment to light a small cigar. As he shook out the match he said, trying to sound casual, "Lily Gail,

41

who is the taller of the two, Clem or Rufus?"

She turned her head and gave him her innocent wide-eyed look. She said, "Why, I don't know, Custis. I've never taken notice. Don't you know?"

He gave her a skinny smile. "I guess I've never taken notice either. Which one of them would you think was the better-looking?"

She gave a little hoot of laughter. "Better-looking? Why, that would be like picking between two mud fences. Better-looking, my stars."

"Lily Gail, would you mind pulling the bedspread over you?"

"But it's so hot." She gave him a look. "I thought you liked to look at me, Mister Long."

"I do," he said. "Generally speaking I do, but right now I'm trying to think. Do either Rufus or Clem have any distinguishing marks?"

Lily Gail gave him a blank look. "What?"

Longarm got up and flicked the sheet a little further over her. He said, "Oh, scars, birthmarks. You know what I'm talking about. Doesn't Rufus have a wart on his nose?"

"Oh, them kind of things. I thought you knew whether or not he had a wart on his nose."

"Whose nose?"

"Why, whichever one you're talking about."

It was like playing checkers with a toddler who couldn't see the board, much less understand the game. He said, "Does one of them have a wart on his nose, Lily Gail?"

"I don't know. You're the one that said it. I've never noticed one before, but then maybe they had it before I knew them."

Longarm was watching her carefully. He knew that Lily Gail had a sly guile about her that made her slippery as a green fish. He knew that if he didn't approach her in exactly the right way, she would catch on and use it to her advantage and try to throw him off the mark.

He said, "I never said either one of them had a wart, Lily Gail. It's been a while since I last saw either one of them. I was just trying to remember their faces. Which one, or either, or both, has something that sets him out?"

"You mean like those there distinguishing marks you were talking about? Like a wart?"

Longarm said, "Dammit, Lily Gail, it doesn't have to be a wart, it can be a scar."

"Well, Rufus has got that big scar along his jaw."

Longarm gave her a look like he thought she was lying. He said in a reproving voice, "Now, Lily Gail, what are you talking about, Rufus having a scar on his jaw?"

"Why, he has. He's got a white scar about six inches long on his jawbone."

Longarm tried to sound doubting. "And where did he get that?"

She said, "You know good and well that his daddy clobbered him on his head with a revolver and laid the flesh of Rufus's face wide open right on that bone. It never did close right and there's that long white scar there."

"That's the left side of his face, isn't it?"

"Of course it is. You know that his daddy was right-handed."

"I seem to remember that now."

"I should think you would."

Longarm narrowed his eyes at her. "How long ago was that, Lily Gail?"

She said, roaming her eyes around the room, "Oh, I don't know, six, seven years, I don't know. Somewhere back then."

He said with an edge in his voice, "Lily Gail, why are you lying to me?"

43

"Well, of all the nerve. We're having a nice conversation and you up and accuse me of lying."

"The reason I'm accusing you of lying is because you are. The last time we discussed this, you told me that you hadn't known the Gallaghers that long. You told me that you'd met them through your husband, and that there hadn't been more than three or four years since you were married to him."

She sat up in bed and got a huff in her voice. "You might well talk about my dead husband, seeing as you are the one that killed him."

Longarm said wearily, "You don't know that I killed your husband and I don't know that I killed your husband. We were chasing that bunch in far eastern Oklahoma, almost in Arkansas, and I shot a man that we have never proven was your husband. You've always claimed I killed your husband because the Gallaghers told you that I killed him, but the Gallaghers may have killed him or he may have just left you. He may be in Mexico right now."

"I'll thank you not to speak of him that way."

"My point is, Lily Gail, that you told me you knew the Gallaghers through your husband."

"That's simply not so," she said. "I've known the Gallaghers ever since I was a little girl, I grew up around them. Why, I've known them fifteen years or so. The very idea, you making me out a liar like that. Where did you ever get such an idea?"

"You told me."

"Well, you misheard, that's all."

Longarm sat back down in his chair, drew slowly on his cigar, and sipped at his whiskey, thinking. It sounded like a true story. He could not imagine Lily Gail inventing a scar made by a man's face being laid open by a blow from a revolver. Longarm had seen such an injury, and when they didn't get stitched up properly, they did leave a long, white, bad-looking scar. He didn't think she was capable of inventing such a story so quick. Given time and research and reason, she was perfectly capable of passing a lie on as truth, especially with those innocent eyes of hers, but it had come out too easily to have been made up so quickly.

He said casually, "Did the Gallaghers say where they wanted to meet me across the line on the strip?"

"Yes, sir, they did. In Quitman, or just outside of it."

"Quitman? That's a boomers' town. I didn't think that place was still standing." He was referring to one of the shanty towns that had sprung up along the Oklahoma line in advance of the land rush that had taken place there. He'd never really understood why the people who had rushed to grab up the free land had been called boomers, but it was a name that suited them well. They had been the dregs of every community from almost every state and territory in the country. By and large, they were either outright crooks or near to the edge. Dollar-grasping, greedy scoundrels who far outnumbered the legitimate farmers who were hoping to find free land where they could make a living and raise a family. The boomers had come through and grabbed what land they could, mostly by chicanery, and then gone moving on to some other rush, be it gold, or land, or whatever.

Longarm said, "Lily Gail, I don't know about Quitman. That's a pretty rough little pueblo, and I reckon about half of that town is related to the Gallaghers through one breed or another."

She said, "They have a sheriff there."

Longarm laughed. "That's a good one, Lily Gail. Now let me take my pants off so you can pull my other leg."

She gave him her look. "Why, whatever do you mean by that?"

45

Longarm said, giving her a level gaze, "Lily Gail, I hope you understand that if the Gallaghers do me serious harm in a way that I won't ever be able to move again, every federal marshal will be looking for them and for you."

She raised half up, causing the sheet to fall away from her breasts. "What do you mean, they'd be looking for me? I have nothing to do with this."

"Lily Gail, don't fool yourself. I've already made known to the right parties that you are the one that contacted me. Now, doesn't that make you want to tell me about this whole setup?"

She turned to face him full on the bed. She said, her face anxious, "Custis, I done told you everything I know. All they told me is to bring their proposition in to you and see what you thought. That's all I know. I don't want no trouble with the United States marshals service."

"When do you expect to meet with the Gallaghers? Are you going to meet with them in Raton tomorrow?"

He could see the uncertainty in her face. "I don't know. I'm supposed to meet someone. I don't know if it will be either Rufus or Clem. I guess they'll get word by either one of the brothers. Why?"

He looked at her for a long moment. "I've got a proposition for them. But if they are not serious about their intentions, then they're just trying to bait a honey trap and you're the bait."

"Now, Custis. That ain't so. I've told you what be the truth as told me."

"We'll see. Now here's what I want you to tell whoever it is that you meet when you get to Raton. You tell them that I will meet one of the Gallagher brothers just across the line on the Oklahoma side toward Quitman. I won't come into Quitman, but I'll meet one of the Gallagher brothers. The other is to come in and stay with a friend of mine named Fisher Lee. I think they will be able to understand that, if I don't get back safe, the brother that will be with Fisher Lee might have some trouble finding his way home. Do you think you can understand that?"

She frowned, furrowing her brow. "No, I don't really get it. Maybe you better tell it to me again."

He took a sip of whiskey. "I think you understand it all right, Lily Gail, but I'll tell you again in the morning just to be sure. What time does your train leave?"

"Ten."

"Then we'll get up at seven so we have plenty of time for you to practice and get your lines straight. Now, we'd better get some sleep. I'm nearly worn out."

Lily Gail said, "You mean, you just want to sleep? Me and you in this nice big bed and you just want to sleep?"

He started undressing. "Lily Gail, I know it's going to be a shock to your system, but that's all I want to do tonight. You stay on your side of the bed."

"I think I'm insulted."

He nodded. "I know this may come as a surprise to you, Lily Gail. There are folks that use the bed for sleeping, and that's just what we are going to do tonight. I'm nearly worn out from fooling around with you and worrying about this other business. The whole matter has taken me unaware, as my body was all prepared to do nothing but rest and have a good time until you came along and brought me this trouble." He sat down on the edge of the bed. "Now, you just stay over there on your side of the bed and we'll make it to morning. Then we'll have some breakfast and get all of our plans straight so that you can understand them. I'll make sure that you get your lines straight."

● ● ●

The next morning at breakfast he said, "Now, your train will arrive in Raton just after noon and you are to meet someone there. You claim that you don't know who, but that's all right. Tell them to get word back to the Gallagher brothers that I'll be at the New Mexico and Oklahoma border tomorrow at about four o'clock. I'll ride on a direct line from Springer to Quitman. As flat as that country is, we ought to spot each other from ten miles off. I'll have a man with me, Fisher Lee. He's a tall string bean of a man, but he's a good man. Now, we're going to stop short of the Oklahoma border and I want Rufus to come across when I cross at the same time."

She looked up from her coffee. "Rufus? You want Rufus?"

He nodded. "Yes, he's the oldest. I think that it's befitting for him to have the nice visit with Fisher Lee." Of course, he didn't tell her that Rufus was the one that she had identified with the scar.

She said, "So, you'll be talking to Clem. What if they don't care for that?"

"Then I reckon the deal is going to be off."

She looked troubled. "They ain't going to like it if I go back and tell them that you're calling the terms. They might blame me for it."

He reached over and patted her hand. "Lily Gail, I have confidence that you can take care of yourself."

"Well, where would this Fisher fellow be taking Rufus, or whoever it is that comes?"

"It's going to be Rufus. I know that Rufus has a scar on his jaw, so they aren't going to try and fool me that way. Rufus and Fisher can come back a mile or two or they can find a shady tree somewhere along the way. The only point is that we want to make sure that I get on back

48

without catching a cold or something else going wrong with me, don't we."

"Custis, you've got it all wrong. I'm telling you that all they want is to get straight with the law. They've got a lot of folks that they are going to put in your hands so that they can make it right."

Longarm said, "Well, you just deliver the instructions that I gave you. We'll be at that line tomorrow afternoon. If they want to play, tell them to be there also and we'll make a swap. Rufus comes into New Mexico and I'll go into Oklahoma."

She furrowed her brow again. "They don't much like to leave Oklahoma."

Longarm nodded. "I know all about that, Lily Gail. I'm not going to ask them to come around law, and I'm not going to ask them to put themselves in some sort of jeopardy, but I'll be damned if I'm going to stick my head into some sort of bear trap without somebody having a damn good hold on the bear. I'm not saying that I don't trust the Gallaghers. It's just that it's a hell of a coincidence to have a bunch of other folks going around robbing and killing and burning down houses and using their name. Kind of makes me suspicious. Explain it to them that way. Right now, it seems like they have something that I may be able to use, but it also appears that I have something they really want and for all I know, what they really want is me and I want to make sure that ain't so. Now, you go back to the room and get yourself ready to go. We need to start for the train depot real quick."

Just before eleven o'clock, Longarm knocked on the door of Fisher Lee's room above the adobe saloon. He'd seen Lily Gail on her train, and watched as it had pulled out for Raton, some seventy miles up the line. It took several knocks before a whiskered, tasseled-haired, and sleepy-looking Fisher Lee finally opened the door. He stood there in summer long underwear, yawning and looking like he'd only had about two hours' sleep.

Longarm said, "My God, man. Do you sleep in those swaddling clothes?"

Fisher Lee blinked his eyes. "What?"

Longarm gestured and said, "That set of underwear you have on. Do you wear that as a regular thing?"

"Hell, Longarm. I don't have much meat on my bones. I get cold."

Longarm asked, "How were you last night? Cold?"

Fisher Lee tried to smooth his hair. "Oh, middling. I probably won a couple hundred, but it wasn't worth the effort. I stayed up until near daybreak."

"Well, that's better wages than sheriffing."

"Yeah, but the hours are longer and the work is harder."

Longarm said, "You ready to talk or do you need a couple more hours of sleep?"

Fisher Lee yawned. "Go on down to that cafe down the street. Let me freshen up and shave and then I'll be on over there as soon as I gather myself up."

Longarm said, "It'll be lunch by then."

"Hell, Longarm, a meal is a meal. It don't make a damn what you call it."

Longarm laughed and said, "My God, Fish, you've turned philosopher in your old age."

"Just go on along and I'll be over there shortly."

Longarm jabbed out a finger. "For God's sakes, change that underwear you're wearing. It's starting to turn green."

Fisher said, "I don't comment on your personal business. I'd take it mighty kindly if you'd do the same for me."

50

"Hurry up."

Longarm clumped down the stairs and went out the door of the saloon.

Fisher Lee ate a half-dozen fried eggs with grits and biscuits while Longarm had a steak and potatoes and some green beans. Longarm said, "Fish, no wonder your head ain't latched on tight with the hours that you keep. You're eating breakfast in the middle of the day. That would be enough to confuse a well man, and you've always just barely been across the border on that score."

Fisher Lee didn't look up. "If there was a body that came up to this table and looked at the both of us and said that one of us had a heavy load on his shoulders, I don't reckon he'd chose me as the one that needed help." He looked up. "And as you are coming to me for help, I'd be a mite slow on those personal criticisms that you have been aiming my way, since I drug my body out of bed for your benefit. Now, would you like to tell me what the situation is and where we're at?"

Longarm said, "Let's get done eating. I never could chew and talk at the same time. This damn situation is more complicated than it seems."

"That woman's involved, ain't she?"

"Yeah, what about it?"

"I don't reckon I need to say anymore. You said it was complicated. That automatically means there's a woman involved."

"Just finish your breakfast."

"You eat your lunch."

They both ate in silence for another fifteen minutes. Longarm pushed his plate away, pulled out a small cigar, and lit it.

51

Chapter 4

Longarm said, "Well, it's this way. Let me tell you what I know, what I think, what I'm planning, and see how much of it you go along with." After that, he told Fish about his idea of having one brother come over while he crossed into Oklahoma to talk to the other one. He said, "I know we talked about it before and we both agreed that we didn't know what the Gallaghers looked like. But I'm willing to trust the description that Lily Gail gave me about the scar on Rufus's jaw."

Fish gave him a skeptical look. "You feel real certain about that, do you?"

"I'm not saying that she is not capable of lying. I'm saying that she couldn't have come up with it that fast and seen the intent behind my questions. I was pretty sly about it."

Fish smiled slowly with his long face. "Yeah, there's been many a man who thought he was sly until he measured his slyness against a woman's slyness. A man's going to come up short every time on that one."

"Well, hell. It's the best that I've got. I don't have any other choice."

"Yeah, you do. You can leave the whole damn situation alone."

Longarm shook his head. "I almost wish I could, Fish, but something inside me won't let me do it."

Fisher Lee shrugged his shoulders and said, "It's your neck. If you want to risk it, that's your business. I'll be glad to ride herd on the one that comes over. If it's Rufus, so much the better. Of course, you still don't know if they're going to take your deal, do you?"

Longarm shook his head again. "No, and I won't know until this afternoon. As soon as Lily Gail gets the word, she is to telegraph me and the business is supposed to happen tomorrow afternoon. I figured that we would have to leave out of here sometime tomorrow morning to get near to the border. We can take the mining company's little train to Springer. That'll knock forty miles off the ride."

"There ain't nothing going to happen unless you hear from Lily Gail?"

"Nothing that I'm going to go along with. If I don't get a hedge on my bet, I'm not about to go along with this scheme, not even if it means a chance to capture the whole damn bunch of them."

Fisher Lee lit a cigarette and shook out the match. "By and by, there's one matter that you've not given all that much thought to. You're going over there and you're not just going to have truck with one of the Gallaghers. There's liable to be a dozen or two of that wild bunch there. What if a few of them have enough of a grudge against you that they don't give a damn what happens to the one that I'm holding? What if they decide to have a party with you, what then?"

Longarm took a sip of the beer that he had allowed to go flat while he ate lunch. "Well, I reckon that I'm a blown-up sucker."

Fisher looked down the street at the people passing by. He nodded toward the windowpane. "Look out yonder at those people taking a stroll through the early afternoon air. There's not a care in the world for most of them. Wouldn't you like to change places with them right now?"

Longarm gave him a sour look. "I had forgotten, Fish, that you always have had a way of sticking a knitting needle right in my most tender parts. Hell, yes. I'd love to be one of them right now. That's what I came here for. I came here to lie around, satisfy a few ladies, win some poker—not your kind of poker, you understand—and get rid of all my troubles and get some relief from all my law work."

His friend looked at him. "Then why don't you do it?"

"Because I can't."

Fisher stood up and shrugged. "I'm going back to bed. I need a nap. Call on me over there at the saloon when you know what's up. I ought to be around somewhere for the balance of the day."

Longarm said, "You still have the underwear on?"

Fisher Lee was about to walk away. He said, "You still not wearing no underwear yourself? Didn't your mother teach you any better?"

Longarm said, "One good thing about not wearing underwear, it takes you less time to get ready."

Fisher Lee said, "Well, you may not have to worry about that much longer."

Longarm gave him a look. "Get the hell out of here. Thanks a lot for that."

No more than two hours later, Longarm was in his hotel room when the clerk brought him a telegram. He went back into the room and sat down on the bed to read it. He was surprised that Lily Gail had managed to act with such swiftness, but then he reckoned that the people she needed to consult were close at hand in Raton. He ripped the envelope open and took the message out.

It was a straightforward enough message, if you didn't consider the source. It said simply that the brothers had agreed to the terms and were willing to meet at the Oklahoma-New Mexico border at a point on a line from Quitman, Oklahoma Territory, to Springer, New Mexico Territory. It was signed Mrs. Baxter.

That gave Longarm a laugh.

He poured himself a drink of the Maryland whiskey and settled in to do some thinking. He sat there, the telegram in his left hand, a glass of whiskey in his right, staring at the four walls. He was trying to visualize all the possibilities. He knew the country, or remembered it well enough, that the basic layout of it was still in his mind. It covered an area from about fifteen miles inside the New Mexico border and then running on into the Cimarron Strip with flat, featureless, unbroken plains. In the summer, it was a sweatbox. In the winter, the wind blew like there was nothing between it and the North Pole except a bony mule. There was very little cover. A man might find a scrub tree or a patch of brush or a depression in the ground or, if he was lucky, a small hummock, but there was no real way that a man could make the ground into his advantage because it was of equal advantage to his enemy. The only good thing that could be said about it was that whoever you were looking for, you could see a long way off. Of course, the person you were hunting could see you, too.

Longarm got up and began pacing the floor, thinking and mulling the matter over. He knew that he could expect to meet quite a few of the Gallagher gang. He wasn't fooled for a moment that they intended to surrender anyone to him. His only ace in the hole was that Fisher Lee would

56

have Rufus. With the meeting time for the following day at four o'clock, they wouldn't have any trouble making such a rendezvous.

The mining company that controlled most of the silver mining ran a little narrow-gauge railway from Taos east into Springer, which was about fifty miles closer. A shuttle train ran almost every two hours beginning at six in the morning. He and Fisher Lee could take that shuttle and leave themselves with the twenty-mile ride in plenty of time to reach the rendezvous by that afternoon. There was a town a few miles inside the New Mexico border. Clayton was its name. He supposed that Fisher Lee could bring Rufus there while he went ahead into the Oklahoma Territory and met with Clem.

In the back of his mind, he wondered if they really thought he was stupid enough to take a dozen of their gang members and promise to leave the brothers alone. But he was quite willing to take the small-fry and quite willing to promise. He just couldn't believe that they were stupid enough to surrender some of their men to him, no matter how ineffective or useless. It had to be that he was the target of the whole plan.

Nothing else came to mind. Why else had they sent Lily Gail with the message? Maybe they really thought he was also stupid enough to be so beguiled by her charm that he could be lured into a deadly trap. He knew he had a reputation as a man who dearly loved the ladies, but if they thought he was willing to get himself killed for one roll in the hay, they had a very dim perception of how he valued his life.

Longarm kept pacing and thinking. What he needed was some sort of an edge, some sort of backup. For the life of him, he couldn't think of what that was. For lack of something better to do, and also because there was a piece of business that needed clarifying, he put on his hat, walked the short distance down to the depot, and got off the telegram to Lily Gail confirming the meeting would take place on the border the next day at four in the afternoon. He asked for an immediate answer.

As he walked back, he noticed the offices of the Silverado Mining Company, which was one of the names the big firm that operated all of the mines in the Taos area went under. Without thinking much about it, he went into the office and asked if he could speak to a mining engineer. A hazy thought had been forming in the back of his mind, but he doubted that it would bear much fruit.

After a few moments, a man came from one of the back offices. He was wearing riding pants with knee-high leather boots and a short leather jacket. He had a amiable face and a short, bristly mustache. He looked at Longarm's badge, and said his name was Simmons and that he was the general manager as well as the mining engineer. He asked how he could help, and invited Longarm back into his office. They sat and talked for a moment about the mining business and how Longarm and Fisher Lee could get their horses on the train. Simmons said he would be happy to give Longarm a note to that effect. "I'm always glad to help out a federal marshal," he said, "especially in this part of the country. You never know when some real law could come in handy."

Longarm smiled. "That's what we're here for, Mister Simmons, to help folks out."

Simmons handed him the note with the instructions to give it to the station manager and they would be taken care of. He asked, "Is there anything else that I can help you with?"

Longarm inched his chair forward and leaned toward the mining engineer. He said, "I need a weapon I think you have and I think you can tell me how to use it. The only problem is that I have to carry it about seventy miles and twenty of it will have to be on a horse. I'm talking about nitroglycerin."

Simmons said, "Are you crazy? That stuff will blow you higher than the moon. I won't say that it is more dangerous than a woman, but it's damn sure more unpredictable. How much nitroglycerin are you talking about?"

Longarm scratched his head. "Well, I don't know for certain. How much would, say, a pint blow up?"

Simmons looked at him thoughtfully. "A pint? Oh, roughly half of this town."

"That much, huh?"

Simmons said, "Marshal, I don't mean to interfere in your business, but nitro is not something that a body should fool around with if they're not extremely experienced with its handling."

Longarm nodded. "Mister Simmons, I appreciate what you're telling me, but if I didn't have a need for this, I wouldn't even consider fooling around with it. I've had experience with dynamite and I know how dangerous that stuff can be."

"Dynamite? Dynamite, Marshal Long, is the equivalent of water to whiskey. Sir, you are talking about a very unstable explosive. Do you know how long our nitro men survive—that is, when we can get them? Obviously, we'd rather use nitro because it blows a lot more ore than dynamite, but nitro men are hard to find. Do you have any idea how long they last?"

Longarm said, his voice low, "Mister Simmons, I'd take it as a personal favor if you'd not tell me. I believe I can get along without knowing that fact. The truth of the matter is, I'm in a hard spot and I have to have a bigger stick than the other fellow, and I can't pack it in a holster and

I can't put it to my shoulder and pull the trigger because there are going to be several more of them than me and I need something that will be a terrific surprise."

Simmons said, "It will be terrific, all right, and it will be a surprise, but just who is going to get the surprise, I wouldn't care to guess."

Longarm said, "I wonder if you could tell me about what amount I could use and conceal that would still pack a pretty good wallop. What about one of those little iodine bottles?"

"Well, that would be about two or three ounces. I'd say that unless you are facing a Mexican army, an amount of that size would be more than ample for your purposes. I have to tell you that I could not allow you to carry that on the train, not ours at least, and I would recommend that you not carry it on anyone else's train."

"Then how am I going to get it to where I am going?"

"We'll transport it for you. There are ways to transport it. One of the safest ways is to pack it in ice."

Longarm said, "Well, that's all well and good. But I have the matter of about twenty miles on horseback. Do you think that your men could pack it down in ice for me? Something that I could carry in my saddlebags?"

"Well, I'm certain we could do that, Marshal, but that ice is going to melt, depending on the temperature of the day."

"How long do you reckon that it would stay cold like that?"

"I don't know for certain. Again, it depends on the temperature of the day and whether you are going to go up into the mountains."

Longarm said sadly, "I ain't going to be going up into the mountains, Mister Simmons. In fact, I'm going to be heading for the hottest part of the state."

Simmons said, "All I can tell you is that the longer you can keep it cold, the better off it will be."

"Mister Simmons, do you reckon that ice could be put in some sort of waterproof container like an oilskin? I'd hate to be riding along and have water dripping out of my saddlebags. The folks that I'm going to be with might take an almighty interest in it."

Simmons nodded. "I don't see where that would be a problem. I do wish, Marshal, you could tell me what you intend to be using this nitro for, but I know that's probably government business and none of mine."

"I'm afraid that's the case, sir, even as obliging as you've been."

Simmons said, "All I can say is that I hope this works out for you. Your name is not unknown to me or to a number a good people in this area, and it's a name that means honesty and integrity and doing the job. I can't say that for the local law we have around here. So it is a worry to me to have one of our finest peace officers contemplating an effort that involves something as unstable as nitroglycerin."

Longarm smiled thinly. "Well, you should have known some of the ladies I have had during the course of my life, if you want to talk about being unstable. But I would just as soon that you didn't make that last statement of yours sound like a eulogy."

Simmons laughed. "Didn't mean it to be so, Marshal. I'm certain that you know what you're doing."

Longarm stood up. "So I can count on that nitro being given to me as I depart the train in Springer?"

"That's correct."

Longarm reached for his wallet. "Let me give you a government voucher for the nitro and for the use of your train, Mister Simmons."

The mining engineer waved off his offer. "That won't be necessary, Marshal Long. The Silverado Mining Company is more than willing to assist duly constituted peace officers in the performance of their duty. I could only wish that your business might include a gang that has been giving us considerable trouble of late. Have you ever heard of the Gallaghers?"

Longarm was in the middle of putting on his hat, and he stayed his arm in midair. "The who?"

"The Gallaghers. Several brothers and a gang of their cohorts."

Longarm looked at the engineer curiously. "What would you be having to do with the Gallaghers? They're mostly in Oklahoma, so far as I know, and they've never done much in the New Mexico Territory."

Simmons said, "Well, actually, they are only minutely into New Mexico Territory. That line you're going to be running on into Springer, we're trying to extend it east past Clayton and join it up to the Missouri-Kansas-Texas railroad line so that we can ship our silver bullion north to government mints. We've been having a problem running the line much further than ten miles out of Springer. Someone just keeps tearing up our tracks."

Longarm looked at him intently. "What does that cause you to do? It doesn't cause you to stack up bullion in Springer, does it?"

Mister Simmons looked surprised. "Yes, in fact it does. We've been shipping the bullion out of here into Springer with the anticipation of sending it on, only that hasn't been possible. Six months ago, we started the line out of Springer with the full intention of having it completed within a month. We haven't laid ten miles of tracks successfully."

Longarm said softly, "Well, I'll be damned. So you're

laying in a good bit of silver ore at the bank or your offices in Springer?"

Simmons said, "Actually, we are converting it into cash as fast as we can ship it out by wagon out to Raton."

"But the wagon shipments are not of any huge value, I take it."

"Quite rightly. We don't send enough silver in one load to make it worth a bandit's time and trouble. Silver is not gold, but we are starting to accumulate quite a bit of cash in our Springer offices."

Longarm looked at Simmons. "Now the M-K-T goes into Raton and then on through the area that you are trying to build through. But you didn't build the line north through Raton because of the mountains in the way, is that correct?"

"Yes, of course. From Springer on, the land is flat. A man would have to be a damn fool to build into the mountains when he could build one on flat ground."

Longarm smiled. "That naturally caused you to build up quite a nice treasure in Springer. One quick raid and the whole pot is gone."

Simmons looked up, puzzled. "I don't quite understand what you are saying, Marshal."

Longarm put on his hat. "That's quite all right, sir, it doesn't matter. I understand and that's all that's necessary. I am much obliged to you for your time and trouble, sir. We'll be getting on the train at eight in the morning."

They shook hands, and then Longarm left the mining office and went walking down the street toward the adobe saloon to find Fisher Lee. His mind was working at a furious pace.

Longarm found Fisher Lee sitting at a back table in the saloon, drinking coffee and smoking cigarettes. Longarm got a bottle of whiskey and two glasses from the bar and went back and sat down at the table. His friend looked up, but made no sign other than the slight tip of his hat.

Longarm nodded toward the coffee. "Having breakfast?"

"I've had breakfast, thank you. Ain't it about time for your supper?"

Longarm poured out two drinks and pushed one toward Fisher. He raised his glass, said, "Luck," and then knocked it back as befitted the toast. Fisher sipped at his.

Longarm said, "I just heard a mighty interesting story from a mining engineer over at the Silverado Mining offices."

"Thinking about branching out into mining, are you?"

"No, I've seen some of the fellows who are mining that silver and it looks a little too much like work to me. Gold, now that's a different story. With gold being worth thirty-five times more than silver, that means thirty-five times less work, doesn't it?"

"You always were a whiz at those mathematics."

"Well, those mathematics, as you call it, are finally explaining some things to me."

"What?"

"What those Gallaghers are really up to."

"Well, are you going to keep it to yourself or are you planning on telling me?"

In a few words, Longarm sketched out for his friend what Simmons had told him. "The way I see it, the Gallaghers are deliberately tearing that track up to force the mining company to stack up a bunch of money there in Springer. They are sending the bullion up in small lots to Raton, not big enough to interest an outfit the size of Gallaghers with the raid of one wagon. They are bringing back cash because cash is easier to store than all that bullion. I doubt they make a safe big enough to store the amount of bullion

64

that Silverado has shipped to Springer."

Fisher's eyes were alive. He drew nervously on his cigarette. "So you figure that they just keep tearing those tracks up, waiting for the pot to build up in Springer before they show their hand?"

"That's correct. They've never showed their hand in New Mexico before to any big extent. It looks to me like they want to make one big raid that's worth their while and get the hell back to Oklahoma."

Fisher said slowly, "I believe that you are on to something there, amigo, but where do you figure to come into this? What's their interest in you?"

Longarm said, "The best that I can figure is that they heard that I was in Taos. They figure maybe I am on to their operation and they don't know that I am here on vacation, or if they heard I was here on leave, they don't believe it. They believe it is a front that I am putting up. They believe that me arriving on the scene about the same time they are about to pull one of their biggest operations has got to be more than coincidence."

"So they plan to get you out of the way?"

"That's the way I see it."

"That leaves one big question."

"What's that?"

"What do you plan to do about it?"

Longarm poured himself another drink, pushed his hat back, and sat back in his chair. "There's the rub, Fish. I ain't at all sure what to do about this. I am on unknown ground against an unseen and uncounted enemy. I've got unknown intentions to deal with—"

Fisher interrupted him. "I don't think there is anything unknown about their intentions. Their intentions are to get you the hell out of the way."

"Maybe so, maybe not. Fish, they haven't been able

to carry on this long without being a little bit smarter than a stump. Do you reckon they're willing to kill a federal marshal in cold blood, knowing the whole entire marshals service would come down on them like a ton of bricks?"

"Well, the story you told me was that they had you chained up in that barn until they could get there to kill you. That sounds like serious intent to me."

"Maybe it was and maybe it wasn't."

"You know this could just be a double opportunity to them," Fisher said.

"Double how?"

"Well, don't forget you killed their brother."

"I didn't kill their brother. The dynamite did it."

"Don't try to call a spade a diamond to me. Who set off the dynamite? It was you. You killed their brother."

Longarm said, "Yeah, but they don't know it."

Fisher gave him another look. "How can you say that?"

"Lily Gail told me that she didn't tell them that it was me."

Fisher slumped back into his chair. "Have you lost your mind, Longarm? Have you got any sort of identification on you? I want to make certain you're really the man I used to know. You're sounding to me like a man who has his head up a pig's ass. You're not seriously telling me that you put stock in that woman's truthfulness, are you?"

"Hell, she ain't smart enough to lie to me."

Fisher said, "I don't believe what I am hearing."

Longarm shook his head from side to side. "That's just it. I'm as confused as hell. I don't know if I believe myself right now."

Fisher said, "Well, there's one thing for certain right now. With this new information you've got, we have to change this about it being just you and me."

"No, Fish. It's got to continue just as it was. I don't know what we are going to do when we get there, but the matter has to be handled the way it has been agreed to by both sides."

"You're not talking to me about keeping your word with that murdering bunch of outlaws, are you?"

"It ain't a question of me keeping my word to them. I wouldn't keep my word any faster than I can spit, but an arrangement has been made that gives me a shot at them and that's all I am looking for. I might have an ace in the hole."

"What kind of ace?"

Longarm shook his head. "I don't reckon that, right now, it's something you need to know."

"If I am going along with you, then anything that involves my neck I most certainly need to know."

Longarm was thinking about the nitro. He said, "Well, I'll tell you at the right time. How's that?"

"When will that be?"

"At the right time."

"I don't much like the sound of that."

Longarm reached over and patted his friend on the shoulder. "What's the matter, Fish? Have you gotten to the point that you don't trust me?"

Fish laughed. "What do you mean, trust you? I never have trusted you. You're crazy."

"Let's go take a walk down to the depot. I want to take a look at the cars on that narrow little railroad they have. I want to make sure they can accommodate our horses in pretty good style."

Fisher got up reluctantly. "I called you crazy a while ago. That's a mistake. I'm the one that's crazy. I got out of law work because I didn't like the hours, the pay, or the work, and here I am planning on getting up at the crack of dawn just so I can be close enough to hear the gunshots when that bunch of cutthroats shoots you."

Longarm was about to walk off when he turned around and looked at Fisher. "What did you just say?"

Fisher said, "What did you have in mind particularly? I said a bunch of things, most of which had to do with me being crazy."

"No, the part about you having to get up at the crack of dawn."

"Well, I will be if we're going to take the eight o'clock train out of here. It takes me a while to get my long underwear on, if you recollect."

Longarm stood there, thinking. Finally, he got out his watch. "It's just a little after three. Go pack your gear and get your horse. We're going to take that six o'clock Silverado huffer-puffer into Springer this evening."

Fisher said, with his mouth wide open, "What? What brought this about?"

Longarm said, "Never mind, just get a move on. I've got a dozen things to do and not much time to do them. Meet me at the depot in plenty of time to load your horse and I'll be there."

With that, he hurried out of the saloon and headed toward the offices of the Silverado Mining Company, hoping that Simmons would still be there.

Chapter 5

Simmons looked slightly bewildered at Longarm's sudden reappearance, but he invited the marshal to come into his office and sit down at his desk. Longarm didn't bother to sit.

He said, "Mister Simmons, do you have a crew right now trying to lay track?"

Simmons shook his head. "I thought you understood that we finally had to shut down. There have been so many raids that we got tired of laying track only to find it torn up the next day."

"Do they attack the crew while they are laying it?"

"Sometimes they do and sometimes they don't. We've had guards out at night trying to keep them away from the track, but they come in such numbers that we haven't been able to stand them off. Marshal, we've had several men killed. We've made appeals to the territorial governor and got nothing, we've made appeals to the sheriff in Springer and got nothing, we've made appeals to the sheriff in Clayton and got nothing. It appears that these outlaws, the Gallaghers, are content that we should build the track about ten miles out of Springer but they don't want it to go any further. There's a butte that rises to the north of our line of march, so to speak, with the track, and they won't let the track go past that."

Longarm said, "Mister Simmons, I want you to have a crew out there at first light tomorrow morning laying track. I want you to try to get past that point that they don't want you to get past."

Simmons shook his head and said, "Marshal, I can't do that. First of all, I'm not sure I can get the men to take the chance, and secondly, I'm not sure that I want to take that responsibility. Like I've said, we've had several men killed and several wounded. I cannot get any help from the local law."

Longarm said, "I'm not local law. I am a deputy United States marshal, and I am guaranteeing you that your men will not suffer any harm. An attack may well happen and if it does, I want them to immediately drop their tools and get the hell out of there. I don't want any attempt on their part to defend themselves. I don't believe that you can hire guards that can stand up to the numbers and ferocity of the Gallagher gang."

Simmons said, "What you say is quite true with reference to the numbers and the fury of the Gallagher gang, but as for the rest, I don't see how you can guarantee it, Marshal."

Longarm said, "Well, sir. This is just a matter that you're going to have to trust me on. Will you put that crew out there laying track in the morning? If you will, I think I can stop your troubles once and for all."

Simmons folded his hands and looked at Longarm for a long moment. "I hope you know what you are asking, Marshal Long."

Longarm nodded. "I'm asking you to fully trust me. You have no reason to. I am asking you to trust me to defend your men against perhaps a dozen or more armed bandits. Yes, I realize what I am asking you."

"Are you by any chance planning on bringing in other deputy marshals?"

Longarm shook his head slowly. "No, sir, I'm not. It will just be me and a friend, the one I told you about."

"Against that gang?"

Longarm nodded again. "I know it sounds like I am stretching it, but if any of your men get hurt, I'll resign from the marshals service."

Simmons laughed. "You don't mean that, Marshal Long."

"If it takes me saying that to convince you that I can do it, I'll say it."

"But will you do it?"

"Of course not. What do you think I am? A damn fool? I'm a deputy United States marshal and I'm about ninety-nine percent sure that I can stop that bunch if they do what I think they'll do. Now, what's your play?"

Simmons sighed and looked out the back window of his office. "I suppose you know what you're doing." He turned around to face Longarm. "All right, I'll wire instructions this afternoon to put a crew back out there laying down track. You said no armed guards?"

"No armed guards. If trouble starts, I want your men out of there in a hurry. I don't care if they are really laying track, I just want them to look like they are laying track."

Simmons looked up at Longarm. "Are you by any chance going to use my crew for bait, Marshal Long?"

Longarm pulled a face and let his eyes drift to the ceiling. "That right there, Mister Simmons, is the very type of question that I don't like to answer."

"Then I'd better not ask it."

"I'd be obliged."

Simmons shrugged. "We're at a stalemate right now. What do I have to lose?"

"You've got a hell of a lot of money to lose in Springer if you don't go along with what I propose."

Simmons looked up at Longarm quickly. "What makes you say that?"

Longarm leaned toward him. "Mister Simmons, think on it for a while. You're a smart man, you've got an education, and I think you'll come up with the answer. Why do you think they are stopping you from building that track on to where you can ship that ore?"

Simmons looked at him for a long moment. "Well, I'll be damned. You know, I believe you're right. Hell, I better get that telegram off right away."

Longarm said, "Just hold up a second. We're taking the six o'clock train, so make sure there's room for us. And Mister Simmons, I know you're going to think that I am crazy, but I want half-a-dozen little one-ounce bottles or vials or whatever you call them of that nitro stuff."

Simmons sat up in his chair. "Half a dozen? Before, you just wanted one."

"Before, I just needed one."

Simmons said, "Then I had better get busy. This is going to take some doing."

Longarm said, "Also, I want there to be a lot of ice where your crew is outside of Springer because I am going to need some to finish my day's work. Follow me?"

"You want my crew to leave some ice where you expect to run into the bandits?"

"Whether I run into them or not, I want there to be plenty of ice to replenish what that nitro has been packed in when it is handed to me."

Simmons said, "It sounds to me that you are starting to gain an understanding of nitroglycerin."

Longarm said, "Has anybody ever had a complete under-standing of it?"

Simmons said, "No, nobody's ever lived that long."

Longarm said as he put on his hat, "That's encour-aging."

He left the mining office and walked directly to the livery stables right behind the hotel. He hunted out the stable boy, a young lad of thirteen or fourteen, and asked him if he knew how to make a slingshot. "You know, one of those things where you take a tree branch that looks like a Y and you use either India rubber or elastic and you've got a little pocket that you pull back to shoot off a rock."

The boy looked at him and said, "Why, yes, sir. That's just as easy as pie. Of course I don't play with them anymore, but I've made a many of them."

Longarm took a coin out of his pocket and said, "I want you to make me one, son. I want you to make me the strongest one ever made and I want you to make it within the next hour. And if you get it done . . ." He took a five-dollar gold piece out of his pocket and spun it in the air. "This is yours."

"Yes, sir. I'll have it made for you in less than an hour."

Longarm yelled after him, "And also, I want my horse at the same time."

Over his shoulder, the boy yelled, "Yes, sir."

Smiling slightly, Longarm walked back up to the tele-graph office, where Lily Gail's telegram confirming the four o'clock meeting time was waiting, and then went back to the hotel, got the key at the desk, and went down to his room. He was about to turn the key in the lock when he realized the door was slightly ajar. With one quick motion, he drew his revolver with his right hand

and shoved the door open with his left. He took one step forward, his weapon out in front of him. He could see the entire room. It was empty except for Lily Gail sitting sedately in a chair by the bed with her frock halfway unbuttoned down her front.

Longarm said, "What in the hell?"

She said, cocking her head prettily, "Why, Mister Custis Long. What a surprise to see you."

With the heel of his boot, he kicked the door shut as he reholstered his revolver. "Lily Gail, what are you doing here?"

She said, "Why, after I got your telegram, there wasn't any other reason for me to stay in Raton, so I thought I'd just come on down here and make sure everything was straight between you and Clem and Rufus and that maybe I would spend the night with you. Isn't that nice?"

He crossed over to her and sat down on the bed. Her dress was unbuttoned enough that he could see the full outline of her right breast. It was a sight that he never could resist. Lily Gail always seemed to wear dresses that unbuttoned down the front. He supposed that she did that for the same reason he didn't wear underwear, but then again, very often she didn't wear underwear either, so she was ready on ready. He reached his hand for the bottle of whiskey and poured himself a small drink. Before he put it to his lips, he said, "I take it that the Gallaghers sent you here to check up on me and see if all was going to go according to their plans?"

She tossed her head and said, "Why, there was no such thing that happened."

"Then how did you manage to be able to return my telegram agreeing that four o'clock was the meeting time? We had talked about it, but it had never been actually confirmed."

74

"Why, I just naturally telegraphed them in Quitman and they telegraphed right back, and then there was this train coming right back here. It was just a little over a two-hour ride, and so I just hopped on board. Just like that."

He nodded with his head. "I see you have changed your dress. This one is blue. Looks very good on you, although with your coloring, I believe yellow is your best color."

"I've got the prettiest little print frock with yellow and blue. I think you'd just love it."

He looked at his watch. It was just past four o'clock. He had, at the most, thirty to forty-five minutes, but of course he definitely didn't want Lily Gail knowing where he was going.

He put his watch away. He reached out his right hand and slid it inside her unbuttoned bodice so he could cup her breasts in his palm. He said, "I don't know about that blue and yellow frock being the prettiest thing I've ever seen. I think this little tittie of yours will do for the time being."

Her breathing was coming quicker now. She said, "Why, you certainly have your nerve, Custis Long."

With his left hand, he unbuttoned the other buttons down her front. As he passed her waist she stood up and shrugged her shoulders, and the frock slid down her body. He reached out his hands and pulled her down next to him, and began very slowly kissing her. He rolled to his left, lying slightly on her.

Lily Gail said, "Honey, your belt buckle is gouging me in the side."

He heaved himself up. "I'll get quit of it." He unbuckled the big silver concave buckle, and then turned his back to her so that she couldn't see that a derringer was hidden inside the buckle, held in place with a wire clip. He dropped his gunbelt to the floor, and then sat down on the bed and took off his boots. With a few swift moves, he shucked off his jeans and turned to her, kissing her again, their mouths open, their tongues thrusting and exploring. After a moment, he slid down and began to take each of her nipples in his mouth.

After a moment, she was quivering and making low moaning noises. She said, "Oh, my. Oh, my. Hurry up, Custis Long, hurry up." With her hands, she was pulling on his shirt trying to bring him on top of her. Just as he got between her legs, with her hands holding and guiding him, there suddenly came a loud rapping at the hotel room door.

A voice yelled, "Longarm, Longarm. Are you in there?"

He swore softly under his breath. Lily Gail moaned and put both of her hands down over the golden patch.

The voice came again. This time, now that the blood had stopped beating so loudly in his ears, he recognized it as belonging to Fisher Lee. Fisher said, "Longarm, dammit, are you there?"

In a strangled voice, Longarm called back, "Yeah, I'm here. I'll be out in just a minute. Hang on. Go down to the bar and I'll be there in ten minutes."

"What are you doing in there?"

"Nothing, just go on down to the bar."

"How come I can't come in?"

"Dammit, Fish, go to the bar, will you?"

"Well, all right, but I need to ask you some things."

"Go to the bar, Fish. You can ask me there."

"You got somebody in there with you?"

"Fish, if you don't get away from that door, I'm going to shoot through it. Do you understand me?"

"All right, dammit. There's no sense of getting all lathered up about it. I'll see you in the bar."

Longarm was still on his hands and knees over Lily Gail. With a sigh, he slowly backed off the bed and stood up. He looked down at her and shook his head slowly. He said, "My, what a waste. Someday I'm going to remember the sight of you lying there like that and I'm going to regret that knock on the door worse than any sound that I've ever heard." He reached out his hand and felt between her legs. It was moist and warm. With a gentle gesture, he ran his finger into her and then pulled it slowly out. "Boy, howdee," he said. "Would I ever like some of that."

She had her eyes closed. Her breathing was beginning to return to normal. She said, "Oh, that bastard. I don't know who that sonofabitch was, but you just go kill him right now."

Longarm said, "I wish I could, Lily Gail, and don't think I don't agree with you that he deserves it." He sat on the edge of the bed and slowly began to pull on his jeans. He buttoned them up, buckled his belt, and then carefully put his gunbelt on, making sure than the .38-caliber two-shot derringer had not been jarred loose from its clip when he dropped his pants to the floor. After that, he pulled on his boots and then stood up. He turned to the woman on the bed. "Lily Gail, I'm going to have to leave for about an hour, maybe an hour and a half. We couldn't finish right now because when a man gets cut off like that, it takes awhile for him to recover. You stay here and keep yourself ready. I'll leave you some whiskey. I have to go off with this man for maybe an hour or so, but I'll be back."

She sighed, "Oh, make it fast, will you, honey? I can't lie here like this, just waiting here for you."

"Maybe you should get dressed and go down into the lobby and give the customers a treat."

Lily Gail asked, "Do you think that would be all right?"

"Yeah, that would be fine." Longarm started moving around the room collecting what he was going to need. He

77

put two bottles of whiskey in his saddlebags and added a clean shirt and a few pair of socks. The saddlebags already contained several boxes of .44-caliber ammunition that fit both his carbine and his revolvers. His extra revolver, the one with the nine-inch barrel, was already in one side of his saddlebags, wrapped in a towel to keep it from banging against things. Lastly, he put on a leather jacket. He knew it would be cold that night where they were going, even as warm as the days were.

Lily Gail opened her eyes and saw him with his carbine in one hand and his saddlebags over his shoulder. She said, "You don't look like you're going off for an hour or two. Where are you going?"

Longarm said, "I've got to help this man pick up a prisoner. That's why I'm taking the rifle. It's a short ride out there, and I'm taking my saddlebags because I've got some manacles and we may have to chain him up."

Lily Gail said, "Oh, so it won't take you long?"

Longarm said, "No, Lily Gail, it won't. I'll be right on back to finish our business and I want you to wait for me as long as it takes."

"All right."

"You promise?"

She said in a small voice, "I promise."

He dug in his pocket, took out a roll of bills, and laid two twenty-dollar bills on the bed. "There's some money in case you feel like buying something or if you get hungry."

"Why, that's ever so nice of you."

"Don't mention it." He gave her a little wave and then carefully let himself out, locking the door behind him and putting the key in his pocket.

Longarm went straight down to the saloon off the lobby, and saw Fisher Lee standing at the bar nursing a beer. He walked up without a greeting and said, "Let's go. We've got a lot of matters to get tended to."

Fisher Lee said, "What are you looking so hot and bothered about?"

"Never mind. Come along, dammit."

Fisher smiled. "I didn't interrupt anything, did I, Longarm? My goodness, I'd hate to think I'd done that to such a good friend like you."

Longarm said, with a vicious look on his face, "Go to hell, you sonofabitch. What prompted you to come over here?"

"Well, it occurred to me that we were going to take a trip and I didn't know how long I was going to be gone, where we were going, and what I would need. So, damned fool that I was, I came over and knocked on your door. Now, wasn't that dumb of me?"

Longarm laughed ruefully. "Well, I guess I can't blame you, but my God, was your timing bad."

"Was you about to have a little picnic, picking some flowers, was you?"

Longarm said sarcastically, "No, I didn't get any flowers, damn you."

"I just feel awful about that," Fisher said.

They went through the big door of the hotel and stepped out onto the boardwalk. Longarm said, "You go on over to the general mercantile and get us some cheese and some saltines and canned peaches, apricots, and whatever else you can find. We'll need provisions for about two meals, and you might get a couple blankets also."

Fisher said, "Now, what in the hell is this? Last I heard we were going to Springer, and I know they have hotels there."

"Yeah, I know, except we ain't staying in Springer. We'll be riding on."

"Damnit, I might have known. You're going to have me out on some dog-ass prairie for two or three days, sure as hell."

"There ain't no use complaining now. Wait until it gets real bad and then you can bitch."

While Fisher headed for the mercantile, Longarm walked over to the mining office for one last visit. Simmons met him in the outer office and they stepped back through the door and out onto the sidewalk.

Simmons said, "I've wired on ahead, and I have a young foreman there who is going to meet you by the name of Eugene Wyman. He is a good man. I wrote the telegram so that he would understand this is a serious matter, but without revealing what your efforts were going to be directed toward. Marshal, I hope you understand about that nitroglycerin. I am sending you with eight one-ounce vials. I am having it packed in fifty pounds of ice on the train. It's being done right now. I hope you understand that the responsibility is yours. I've also wired Eugene some instructions about that. Is it my understanding that you are going to be pushing on from Springer tonight by horseback?"

"That's correct, although I don't remember saying it."

Simmons smiled. "Well, I have the feeling that you plan to be somewhere near the end of our tracks tomorrow morning, and if that's the case, you'll be doing some traveling tonight."

Longarm said, "Very good, just don't let it get around."

"I understand. I want you to know that anyone who works for the mining company is at your disposal. Anything you need, anyone need, ask Eugene and he'll see that you have it. He is going to round up a crew for you. He will assure them there will be no danger, and I hope that's true."

Longarm said, "I'm going to make it as true as I can. I want to thank you, Mister Simmons, for your assistance." He put out his hand. "I think it will turn out all right."

Simmons said, "Sounds kind of risky to me, but then, risk is your game."

Longarm smiled. "Aren't you the one that plays around with nitro?"

Simmons laughed ruefully. "Yeah, I hope you understand I get paid damn well for it."

"I intend to get paid for it also." After Longarm left Simmons, he walked over to the livery stables. He wasn't quite to the door when the young man he'd hired to make the slingshot came rushing out, holding the very instrument that he had been assigned to create in his hand.

"Here you go, mister. Now, isn't this a beauty? It's got two two-foot-long India rubber bands on it, and look how soft this pouch is. It'll hold a good-sized stone. Look here, I peeled the bark off of the Y branch. Ain't that a beauty?"

Longarm took the slingshot by the handle, pulled the pouch back tentatively, stretching the thick rubber bands, and aimed between the Y of the two arms of the slingshot. He said, "Son, you did good. This is fine." He reached into his pocket, took out the five-dollar gold piece, and flipped it in the air. The young man jumped two feet off the ground to catch it. Longarm laughed. "Good job, son. Now, you can fetch me my horse and saddle and I'll be ready to go."

The young man turned, saying, "Yes, sir!" and ran back into the barn.

While he and Fisher were waiting, Longarm speculated on why Simmons had decided to give him eight vials of the nitro instead of the six he had asked for. For a moment, the answer seemed simple: The extra two would be replacements in case he broke a couple. But then the thought occurred to him what would happen if he broke even one of them—he wouldn't need the other six. He wouldn't need anything. After he got through shuddering at the thought, it occurred to him that Simmons had a fair idea that he was going to use the nitro in some fashion against the Gallaghers, and had decided that if six ounces were good, eight were better. In some ways, Simmons was a very astute man.

They were sitting in a stock car with both of their horses loaded. Longarm had brought along a dun that was part quarter horse and part thoroughbred, a horse he had paid three hundred dollars for, which he thought was a considerable sum. The dun was a big, quick, barrel-chested horse that had good staying power. He had been one of the best horses Longarm had run across in the hundreds of horses, perhaps thousands, that he had gone through in his lifetime. Longarm had noted that Fisher had a sleek-looking black that appeared to have some good breeding in him, but then that was Fisher. Fisher liked the best. At that moment, he was sitting next to Longarm in a white silk shirt and the soft leather vest that he'd had on the night before.

Longarm said, "You're going to wear those kind of clothes to sit in a stock car full of dust and straw?"

Fisher gave him a look. "They're the only kind of clothes I got. Besides, what's one silk shirt more or less?"

The car seemed uncomfortably small, although there was plenty of room for the horses and the two men. The narrow-gauge railway was simply that; the rails were placed ten inches closer together than normal rail tracks, and the cars were sized accordingly. The mining company used the stock car because they used donkeys, burros, and mules in their mines and they were constantly shipping them around. The train looked smaller only in comparison to the other trains sitting in the depot. The engine looked, to Longarm, like what the railroad called a switching engine, one that was used around the freight yards to switch cars from one siding to another.

Not long after they had arrived at the train and gotten their horses loaded, a man in working clothes had pulled Longarm aside and inquired if he was the marshal. Longarm hadn't been wearing his badge, and he had pinned it on for answer. The man had said, "I've got your goods in a car up the train. Got them well iced down in a swing cradle. They ought to be all right."

Longarm had said, "Just out of curiosity, what if they aren't all right? You said they *ought* to be all right, but you didn't say for sure."

The man had spat tobacco juice reflectively to one side. "Well, that's the one good thing about nitro. If you make a mistake with it, you'll never find out."

Longarm had said, "I can't tell you how much that comforts me, mister."

Now the train began a series of slow jolts as the engine moved off and the slack was taken up in the coupling. Longarm said, "Looks like we're moving." He took out his watch. It was six o'clock on the button. "It seems the mining company runs their trains on a tighter schedule than the regular lines."

Fish said, "Yeah, that would be handy if I knew where the hell we were going and what the hell we are going to do."

Longarm said, "Fish, you play five-card stud, don't you? Isn't that one of your favorite games?"

"I put it on a par with draw—five-card draw—it's all serious poker."

"Well, what I'm getting to is that you get a card up and then you get a card down, which you bet on, and the others either call or fold, and then you have to wait for the next card, don't you?"

"Yeah."

"Well, that's what you're doing right now. You're waiting for that next card."

Fisher said, "I have a feeling that this trip is going to wreck my health. You know a man of my age and sensibilities needs to keep to a regular schedule. You done woke me up way early this morning and got my feeding habits out of kilter, and now here we are riding a train through the mountains to some damned town in New Mexico that I didn't want to be in, and I've got a feeling that we are going to get on horseback and ride on tonight. How many other surprises am I going to get?"

Longarm said, "Well, every new card is a surprise, isn't it, Fish?"

"Yeah, but I can fold my hand if the one I get doesn't work and I don't care for it."

"That's the difference between this and poker. You've got to stay until the end of the pot; you can't fold this hand."

Fisher yawned. "Longarm, did anybody ever tell you that you're a circular sonofabitch?"

"Okay, I'll bite. What's a circular sonofabitch?"

Fisher gave him an eye. "That's a sonofabitch anyway you look at it."

The train slowly made its way out of Taos and started winding through the mountains that ringed the valley where the town was located. With agonizing slowness, the train chugged its way up steep inclines and around bends that were too sharp for Longarm's comfort. Occasionally, the train would rumble, jarring over a patch of rough roadbed,

84

and Longarm's senses would tingle as he thought of the eight ounces of nitro swinging in the cradle somewhere up ahead.

The roadbed, as it climbed through the mountains, was so narrow that Longarm could lean forward in the narrow stock car and see through the slats in the side to the bottom of the valley a thousand feet below. He said, "Boy, I hope this train is made out of some kind of light material."

"How come?"

"So when we jump the tracks and fall all the way down, we won't make such a racket when we hit."

Fisher said, "That's a hell of a nice thought. You got any more information that you want to give me?"

Longarm reached into the pouch of the saddlebags and brought out a bottle of his Maryland whiskey. He pulled out the plug and offered it to his friend. Fisher took a small drink, a sip, and handed it back.

Longarm asked, "You never have been much of a drinker, have you, Fish?"

"Never have seen the need. It never did much for me and I could see where it caused some folks a good deal of harm. I ain't got nothing against it. You appear to enjoy taking a drink, but I just don't. Have you ever eaten a raw oyster?"

Longarm said, "Yeah, but only once. I was in Baltimore for some kind of trial that I had to testify in, and this lawman got me out to dinner and insisted that I eat one of those nasty things."

Fish said, "He probably told you that it was something that if you ate enough of you'd like, right?"

"Yeah."

"Well, that's the way I feel about whiskey. I don't think it's worth the effort."

Longarm looked out at the snowcapped mountains they were winding their way through, feeling it getting cooler and cooler with every foot they climbed. He said, "You know, Fish. You never really gave me a good reason why you quit the law business. I don't believe it was because you could make more money playing poker."

"No, that was never it. It wasn't the danger, matter of fact, it was the lack of danger. What do you think of your average criminal, Longarm? Not people like the Gallaghers, but just your average idiot that sets out to rob a bank?"

Longarm shrugged. "Not a hell of a lot. Most of them ain't a real hand with a gun."

"Exactly. I've never really discussed this with anybody before, but I've got to tell you this, Longarm. I got to feeling ashamed. The damned fools wouldn't admit when they were whipped, when they were in over their head. Some stupid farmer who couldn't make a living suddenly thought he could walk into a bank with a pointed gun and they would give him all the money. Then when the law came looking for him, he thought he could beat them, but he forgot that a gun was the lawman's stock in trade. There was just too many times, Longarm, when I felt I was committing murder. It's just that simple."

Longarm nodded. "I know what you mean, Fish, but if they haven't got sense enough to drop the gun, you've got to do what you've got to do. Hell, a blind sow can find an acorn, so you're liable to catch a stray bullet, and a stray bullet will kill you just as quick as a well-aimed one."

They rode on in silence for another quarter of an hour. Longarm had a good drink of whiskey, corked the bottle, and put it back into his saddlebags before lighting one of his small cigars. He said, "The Gallaghers ought to be on their way right now from Raton to somewhere on the Cimarron Strip."

Fish looked around at him. "How do you know that?"

"Because Lily Gail showed back up unexpectedly. I sent a telegram to confirm the meeting and the time, and she damned near got back before the return telegram arrived."

"Did she say the Gallaghers were in Raton?"

"Oh, hell, no. She said she had wired them in Quitman, Oklahoma, and that they wired her back with the details, and that they were acceptable the way I proposed that we do it."

Fish laughed slightly. "Hell, Quitman ain't got no telegraph office."

"I knew that, but I didn't mention it to her. I figure they left and she didn't have a good reason to hang around Raton, or else they sent her back down to check on me. Anyway, I've got a pretty good idea of how this thing is falling out."

Fisher gave him a grin. "So, that's who was in there when I was knocking at your door. Right?"

Longarm said, "I don't calculate that would be any of your business, Mister Lee."

Fisher Lee, still grinning, said, "You were having yourself a little hair pie, weren't you?"

Longarm gave him a glare. "I was about to have myself some hair pie until a so-called friend of mine came along and upset the kettle."

Fisher kept grinning. "Well, I am just tore up to hear that, Mister Custis Long. That purely twists my heart to know that I caused you the hardship and the loss that you've suffered."

Longarm said, "Oh, go to hell."

After a pause Fisher said, "You know, sooner or later, you've got to tell me what the plan is. I'm not going to just follow, so if you'd like to enlighten me . . ."

Longarm said, "I wish to hell I really knew what the plan really was, but a lot of it depends on how the Gallaghers react. But I can tell you this. You and I are going to get off this train in about twenty or so minutes and unload the horses, and then take off east for ten or fifteen miles. We're going to get on top of some high ground and bed down for the night and see what comes our way."

Fisher Lee cursed silently and softly for a moment. "Dammit, Longarm. I vowed to myself when I had gotten out of law work that I had slept on the ground for the last time."

"Nobody says you have to sleep on the hard ground."

"Oh, yeah? Where in hell else am I going to sleep?"

"Well, you've got lots of choices. You can sleep standing up, you can sleep leaning against a rock, you can burden your poor horse and sleep in the saddle all night. Hell, what are you complaining about?"

"You're going to get yours one of these days. I'm going to get you one of these days, Longarm, hopefully in a poker game. I'm going to turn you every which way but loose. I'm going to take all your money, then I'm going to take all your property, then I'm going to take your nest egg that you've probably got buried in a tin can in your backyard, then I'm going to take all your women, and then finally I'm going to take every damned gun you've got and then challenge you to a duel."

Longarm said, "Fish, you've got to quit taking these things personally. You're a bigger man than that."

Fisher spit toward the slat, but the wind whipped it toward the back of the car. "Folks have been picking on me all of my life just because I am skinny. I want you to know that I'm not skinny, just wiry, and there is a big difference, as you will find out before this trip is over."

Longarm said, "That hurts me, especially after the way that I've been defending you here lately."

"What do you mean, defending me lately?"

88

"Why, there in Taos. There were folks that said that you bayed at the moon and cheated at cards. I told them that you did not bay at the moon."

Fisher gave him a look.

The train pulled into Springer about an hour after dark. Once they had come out of the mountains, it had warmed up considerably. At one time, as they were going through the highest pass, Fisher had felt compelled to wrap himself in a blanket, noting that slim folks tended to get colder than those with a lot of fat on their bones. They'd come chugging in on the train, switching off to a siding that went directly to the complex where the mining company's headquarters were located in Springer.

After they had detrained and gotten their horses off, a young man dressed very much like Simmons came forward to Longarm and identified himself as Eugene Wyman. He drew Longarm a little way off from Fisher and said, "Marshal, your goods are being transferred now. What I am going to do is load them on one of our little mine burros. We've got a canvas contraption rigged up that will hold fifty pounds of ice in each pocket. We've got four vials each of the hot stuff per pocket. I do want to warn you. I don't know how far you are going, but even with that fifty pounds of ice, it is not going to last much longer once it starts getting warm tomorrow. We will have some ice down there at the end of the rails when we send the crew, and we will be able to replenish your supply. You should have enough to last you through the night, but I'm sure Mister Simmons has told you that it's a lot better to keep that stuff cold."

Longarm said, "Mister Simmons has made his point and I'm much obliged to you. Why a burro?"

The young man smiled. "The burro is an old hand that

we've had a long time. His name is Pedro and he is as surefooted as a mountain goat. I can assure you, Marshal, that the last thing that you want to happen when you're carrying the kinds of things that you are carrying is for the animal to stumble with such a load. Anybody within half a mile would just as soon not have that animal stumble, and I think you will come to appreciate old Pedro before your trip is over."

Longarm said, "I appreciate him now."

"We should have you ready to travel in about half an hour. We've got a kitchen over here that is reserved for our workers. Maybe you'd like to take some supper before you set out."

Longarm said, "That sounds like a capital idea. In fact we brought some provisions along with us, but I could use a hot meal anyway. We are going to be setting up as high as we can find a place, but I imagine it gets pretty chilly up on this high plain, even in the summer."

"You know it. You'll need more than one blanket."

"Well, maybe you'll loan us a couple, three more?"

"I'll see that that's tended to. Now, if you and your friend will follow me, I'll take you over to the cookhouse, and someone else can see to your horses and when you come out, you'll be ready to travel."

Longarm said, "That suits me fine."

Fisher was delighted that they were going to have a good meal before setting out across the plains of eastern New Mexico. He said, "I was beginning to figure, Longarm, that hanging around with you was a quick way to ruin my health. At least we'll have a meal before we probably get ourselves killed."

Longarm said, "As skinny as you are, it doesn't take that much to feed you."

In the cookhouse they made a good meal of steak and

potatoes and apple pie. By the time they were outside and mounted up, Fisher seemed content for a change. As they got ready to start out of the camp Eugene appeared, leading a small burro with a double pack on his back. He handed the lead rope to Longarm and said, "I'm sorry, Marshal, but I reckon that you'll have to accommodate your pace to that of Pedro's, and he is none too swift."

Longarm said, "That's quite all right with me, just as long as he is as sure-footed as you say he is."

"You can depend on that."

"I take it that we just follow this set of narrow-gauge tracks?"

"Yes, sir. That'll take you to exactly where you want to go."

"See you in the morning."

As they trailed slowly out of the camp and out of the town of Springer following the railroad tracks, Longarm could tell that Fisher was about to bust to know what the burro was for and what he was loaded down with. His pack was two well-secured canvas sacks that hung down on each side. The sacks were covered with canvas to hold in the cold of the ice and to keep it from melting any sooner than it had to. They had gone about a mile when Fisher said, "All right, damnit, what's the burro for and what's he hauling?"

Longarm answered, "Ice."

Fisher asked, "What the hell is the burro hauling, Longarm? What's in those big saddlebag-type canvas bags?"

"Ice."

"Dammit, Longarm. Are you going to tell me truth or not?"

Longarm swiveled around in his saddle to face Fisher. "I am telling you the truth. Lean down there and feel—

real gentle, though—the side of that canvas and see if it ain't cold."

Fisher said, "I'll do no such thing, but if it's ice, do you mind telling me why in the hell you are carting ice with us?"

Longarm shrugged. "I thought we might make some ice tea or some lemonade."

For a half minute, Fisher Lee swore loudly and effectively. Then he said, "All right, don't tell me, see if I give a damn."

Longarm said, "You don't want to know."

"Why don't you let me be the judge of that?"

"Because after you know, you won't want to know."

"Then you're saying that I don't want to know."

"Yeah."

"Well, that's a hell of a note. Here we are riding toward some kind of rendezvous with God only knows how many bad-assed characters, we're going to be overwhelmingly outmanned and outgunned, we don't know the terrain, and now you're telling me there is some more bad news that I'd be better off not knowing. Hell, Longarm, you're just a pure comfort to a body."

After half an hour, they were well clear of the town and the moon was up good in the eastern sky. They crossed the small foothills of the mountains they had just traversed, and began entering the broad flat plains that stretched out in all directions to Texas, Kansas, Oklahoma, and beyond. Off in the distance they could see, here and there, the buttes rising from the flat arid land. Some of them rose up sheer to heights of five and six hundred feet. Some were rounded and some jagged and rock-strewn.

Longarm said, "A butte is a marvelous thing. Don't you agree, Friend Fisher?"

"One of nature's works. I wonder if you, my high-ranking government official, truly appreciate the butte and how it came to be?"

"Well, I don't know that I ever studied on the question," said Longarm. "I reckon an answer will come to me, given time. However, if you happen to know, I've got nothing better to do than to lead this burro and ride alongside this track and listen to what you do know about them."

Fisher said, "Well, in spite of my curiosity about that load of ice that burro's carrying, I'm willing to tell you about the butte because it is a work of nature. A marvel. At one time, this very land that we are riding on was as high as any of the tops of those buttes you can see."

Longarm said, "Oh, come on, Fisher. Be serious."

"It is a fact. It is a testimony that granite and quartz are harder than sandstone."

"Hell, everybody knows that."

"Well, then you ought to know how a butte was formed. Millions of years ago, notice I said millions of years ago, all this territory that we are looking at was flat."

"Bullshit."

"No bullshit to it. This territory was all the same height. Then, through all those millions of years, through wind, rain, and erosion, caprock of quartz and granite covered those buttes and protected the sandstone beneath it. When the wind and the rain swept the sandstone and the limestone and the dirt and the sand away from parts that were not protected by a caprock of hard rock, the buttes were formed. They were not formed so much as they withstood the ravages of nature."

Longarm looked over at him. "You've been reading those books again, haven't you, Fish? I've warned you about that. Not only will it weaken your shooting eye, it will also put wild ideas into your head. I recommend that you take up drinking and give up those books."

"Say what you will, my friend, but the butte is a lonely sentinel to the durability of the caprock. While all the rest of this material that used to be here was being washed and blown away, that caprock of hard quartz and granite protected each one of those buttes. So there they stand. They didn't rise up, they simply would not go down."

Longarm asked, "Are you to have me believe that all this dirt and sand and limestone and the other softer rocks were washed away and blown away to somewhere else?"

"I am willing for you to believe that."

"Well, you're going to have to tell me where it went to because I haven't seen any of it piled up."

"Ahhh . . . but you weren't here millions of years ago to see it redistributed. You haven't considered that, Longarm. You think a long time ago was the last time you had a piece, even if it was this afternoon."

"You better quit bringing that up, Fisher, if you have any sense."

"Anyway, that's the story about how buttes came to be formed."

"Well, that's going to do us a hell of a lot of good tomorrow if we get in a gunfight with the Gallaghers. I'll yell down at them and tell them that you know how the buttes were formed, and that will probably make them drop their guns and head for home."

Fisher shook his head slowly. "He that will not learn, cannot learn. You are doomed to eternal ignoramusness, Longarm."

"My God, I wish we'd get to the end of this line. If I have to listen to much more of this clabber, I'm liable to begin talking like you."

They trailed along through the quiet night, the only sound being the soft shuffle of their horses' hooves in the sandy dirt. Every now and then, a horseshoe would

94

strike a rock and make a *clink,* but other than that and
the occasional howling of a far-off coyote, there was little
noise to hear. Pedro, the burro, came along docilely as if
he had been trailing across the prairie for most of his life.
To keep up with the walk of the horses, he had a trotting
gait that had at first alarmed Longarm, but as soon as he
was able to see that it didn't jostle the load, he was content
that Pedro knew his job.

Finally, they came to the end of the line. They had been
riding for perhaps two hours. Longarm calculated it to be
sometime after ten o'clock. They identified the end of the
line by the lengths of twisted tracks and piles of burned
cross-ties lying about.

Fisher said, "Looks like somebody is trying to hold up
progress here."

Longarm said, "Guess who?" Off to his left, he could
see a tall butte about half mile distant. He took that to be
the one that Simmons had said the Gallaghers would not
let the track pass. He turned his dun to the left and toward
the butte. They had left the mountains, but there were
some small rises, and here and there small groves of trees.
Looking at the butte from a distance, Longarm wasn't
sure how far up it they could get their horses. He figured
Pedro could make it, but he wasn't sure about the bigger
horses.

Longarm led them to the butte, which appeared to be
about two or three hundred feet high and about a quarter
of a mile across, and then led them around to the back.
About a hundred yards from the foot of the big structure,
there was a clump of trees.

Longarm said, "Fish, I think we'd better tie our animals
here and make it on foot the rest of the way."

"I take it by making it on foot the rest of the way that
you are talking about getting on top of that butte."

"That's what I have in mind. I think we're going to need the high ground, and that appears to be as good as we're going to find around here."

Fisher asked, "Have you ever climbed one of these things?"

"No, can't say that I have."

"Well, you are in for a treat."

They rode into the grove of trees and dismounted. They loosened the cinches on their horses' saddles, then took the bits out of the animals' mouths and tied them to some low branches so that they could graze on what little grass was there. Longarm said, "They're not going to have a real good night of it, but that can't be helped. They got plenty of feed and water on the train coming up, so I guess they'll just have to be patient."

Fisher asked, "What about old Pedro there?"

"He'll be going with us." Longarm untied his saddle-bags and slung it over his shoulder. He said to Fish, "I hope you brought plenty of ammunition."

Fish gave him a look. "Going out on a job with you? No, it never crossed my mind."

Longarm chuckled. "I've got four boxes of .44-caliber shells."

"I can match that and then some."

"You got the grub?"

Fisher patted one pouch of his saddlebags and said, "I'm all set."

Together they trudged out of the little copse of trees and walked over the sandy, rocky ground. Longarm carried his carbine in one hand and led Pedro with the other.

When they got to the foot of the butte, they ranged left and right, looking for an easy trail up. There didn't seem to be any.

Longarm said, "Fish, why don't you go on ahead and

find the best route and I'll try to follow you with this burro."

Fisher said, "That burro is the one that ought to lead. I imagine he knows more about this kind of climbing than you and me."

In the still cool of the night, which was getting colder by the moment, they began working their way up the butte. It was broad enough at the base that the first hundred feet or so were not much trouble. Pedro came along easily, having no trouble, even where the men's boots slipped and they were forced to their knees. After that it was harder. Longarm and Fisher were reduced to leaving their rifles behind so that they would have their hands free to pull themselves along. At a height just below the crest, they found a wide ledge that looked out onto the flat land below. In the moonlight, Longarm could see the gleam of the narrow-gauge tracks. There was a jumble of rocks on the ledge between them and the edge, big enough to hide the burro and well-placed enough to give them shooting positions.

Longarm said, "This ought to do."

Fisher said, "I'll go back and get the rifles. You might want to get that donkey unpacked. By the way, where are the blankets? I brought three and gave them to that Eugene fellow down in Springer to go with some more that he had. Hell, it's getting as cold as all get-out."

Longarm said, "I don't know. Maybe they're packed in with that ice Pedro is carrying."

Fisher gave him a look. "Oh, that's a nice place to put blankets. On ice. That's one hell of a way to keep warm. Someone ought to be proud of that kind of thinking."

Finally, they established their camp under the protection of the rocks. Pedro stood patiently against the wall of the butte, perhaps grateful to have his load of ice removed.

Longarm had taken it off by himself, being extremely careful, calculating that it was the heaviest hundred pounds he had ever lifted in his life. He'd carried it away and put it behind a big boulder. He didn't think that it would matter much if eight ounces of nitroglycerin decided to go off, but somehow having it out of sight like that made him feel better.

The blankets indeed had been packed on top of the ice. He'd taken them out carefully and then spread them on the rocks. Only the undersides of two of them were cold. They'd warm quickly.

Fisher said, "I don't reckon we can make a fire."

"No, I don't reckon we can. What were you going to do? Fry that cheese or heat up a can of peaches?"

"I just find a fire sociable, Marshal Long, if it's not too much trouble for you to comprehend."

"Let's get our bedrolls made and then settle down. You can sleep if you want to. It's about eleven-thirty."

Fisher said, "Strangely enough, I don't feel sleepy."

"You ought not to be hungry either. How many steaks did you eat back there at that cookhouse? Three?"

"Two. The same as you."

"I didn't know you were counting."

They got settled under the night sky, each man taking three blankets. It had now turned seriously cool. Longarm calculated the temperature was in the low forties. If it had been noon, the temperature would been nearly ninety degrees, but that was the desert for you. He knew it would get colder before dawn. For a time he sat, like Fisher, on one blanket with the other two shrouded over his shoulders. A thought occurred to him, and he went to his saddlebags and got out a bottle of whiskey and the slingshot. He went back and offered Fisher a drink.

This time Fisher said, "I believe I will. Of course, you

98

understand, this is for medicinal purposes. To help fight off the cold."

"Yeah, and rattlesnake bites."

Fisher took a drink and passed the bottle back.

Longarm settled himself, had a drink, put the cork back in the bottle, and began examining the slingshot. There were a few small rocks lying nearby, and he put one in the leather pouch. He drew back the rubber bands and let fly into the night. He could see the stone curve well out into the flat land below. He lost it after it dipped below the horizon, but he could see that the slingshot was capable of carrying at least a hundred fifty to two hundred yards. It was going to make a very satisfactory weapon.

Fisher looked at him in astonishment. "What in the name of hell have you got there?"

"Ain't you ever seen a slingshot before?"

"Yeah, I've seen a slingshot before, but I don't recollect ever seeing a grown man with one, especially a grown man that's out on some fairly serious business. Are you going bird hunting or squirrel hunting? What do you plan to do with that thing?"

Chapter 6

Longarm picked up another stone and fired it high into the night sky, admiring the arc it made. He said, "Oh, I reckon to kill me a giant."

"Hell, who do you think you are? David? Ain't nobody around here named Goliath."

Longarm said, "This, my friend, might be the most deadly weapon you've ever seen."

Fisher shook his head slowly. "I'm sitting on top of a rock with a crazy man wearing a badge who's got a kid's slingshot, and we might have two dozen armed bandits coming this way at first light. Can you beat that? You know, for years, I have told people that my mamma didn't raise no fool. I was wrong, because here I am."

Longarm said, "Don't be too hard on yourself. You're still alive. I don't know how, but you are."

"And another thing, when in the hell are you going to tell me what that ice is for? You plan on dumping it down this butte and freezing those folks to death?"

Longarm said, "I'm keeping something cold." He had about decided that it was time that Fisher knew what his plan was. He had gotten this far, and Longarm was pretty certain that Fisher would stay.

Fisher asked, "Exactly what do you need to keep cold?"

Longarm said, "Do you promise not to get nervous if I tell you?"

"Well, I don't know what you could have sitting on ice that would make me nervous, unless it was that woman that you had in Taos. She sounds like she could use some cooling down. Yeah, I promise I won't get nervous."

"No matter what it is?"

"No matter what it is. I don't think there is anything more that you could do or say to me in the history of our acquaintance that would make me nervous. I've been through the wars with you, Longarm, and I've been in some places that I swore that I'd never get into, and I got into them because of you, and I'm still here. What do you have in the ice?"

Longarm looked around at Fish so he could see his face fairly distinctly in the moonlight. He said, "Nitro."

Fish blinked. "What?"

"Nitroglycerin."

Fish made a sighing sound. "Are you telling me that you packed some nitroglycerin on the back of that burro all the way from Springer with me riding right next to it? Are you going to tell me that, huh?"

"Not if it's going to make you nervous."

Fisher swallowed, his Adam's apple bobbing prominantly. He said, "You mean, on that banging, swaying, jerking, bucking train there was some nitroglycerin? That stuff that goes off if you even breathe on it wrong?"

"That very stuff. Nitroglycerin. Highly unstable. The secret is keeping it cold, Fish. Even then, there ain't no guarantee."

"Am I to understand then that sitting over there behind that boulder in those canvas sacks full of ice there is some nitroglycerin in there, not ten yards from where I am sitting?"

Longarm nodded. "Yes."

Almost imperceptibly, Fisher began to back away. "You got just a little bit, right?"

"Not very much."

Fisher was easing himself backward, using his hands to slide his rump along the rock ledge. "What do you mean, not much?"

Longarm gave him an innocent look. "Oh, eight ounces."

Fisher's chin slumped to his chest. He said, "Lord, I am ten yards from eight ounces of nitroglycerin and I'm here with a madman, a crazy man. Please get me somewhere else, a long way away somewhere else."

Longarm said mildly, "I didn't know you were a praying man, Fish. I'm right pleased to find it out. That just goes to prove that there is good in everything, even nitroglycerin. I might have gone on to believe you were a benighted heathen, and now I know better."

Fisher glared at him. "Longarm, you are the lowdownest, dirtiest sonofabitch that I have ever known in my life. You let me walk right beside, ride right beside, enough nitroglycerin to have blown you and me and all the animals to Connecticut, and now I'm sitting ten yards from it. Longarm, I'm scared of that stuff."

"So am I. Anybody with a lick of sense would be scared of it."

"Well, what are you going to do about it?"

"I'm not going to go over there and shake it, if that's what you mean."

Fisher gave him a sour look. "You know damn good and well what I mean. What are you going to do about it?"

Longarm shrugged. "I'm going to let it be. If I was you, I'd do the same. It's nice and safe in that ice."

"Yeah, it's nice and safe in that ice, but what about when that ice melts underneath it and it falls?"

Longarm had not thought of that, and it sent a sudden chill through him. "There you go, Fisher, always thinking the worst. That nitroglycerin is packed on the bottom, the ice is on top of it, so it can't fall. It's carefully wrapped. The men that put that nitro together for us are mining engineers. They deal with this stuff all the time, so they know exactly what they are doing."

Fisher asked, "Are you sure of that?"

Without the slightest idea that what he was saying was true, Longarm said, "Of course I'm sure. It was explained carefully." He said it with conviction, but the thought of the ice melting below one of the vials and allowing it to suddenly slide down and hit the rock ledge was nearly more than he could bear. It didn't matter that he was slightly closer to the nitroglycerin than Fisher. All that meant was that he might have one millionth less of a second to live than Fisher. He put on an elaborate yawn. He said, "Fisher, the trouble is not tonight. That stuff is cold in that ice and it's cold outside. We haven't got a thing to worry about. Our trouble is tomorrow when the Gallaghers show up. And of course, if they don't show up, that's real trouble."

"If they don't show up it's trouble? You want to explain that to me?"

"That means we have to go get them."

Fisher stuck out a finger. "No, that means *you* have to go get them. At first light, I've discharged my responsibilities and I'm getting on my horse and I'm heading right back to Taos."

Longarm shook his head sadly. "I'd hate for word to get around that you let a friend down, Fish. A lot of people would find that hard to believe of you."

Fish said, "Not when they find out what you've done to me, they won't."

Longarm said mildly, "As far as I can tell, Fish, I haven't caused you the slightest bit of trouble. I've brought you on a nice train ride, and here we are out in this beautiful country on a beautiful night. We've got a bottle of whiskey, although I know you don't care much for it, but it's still a very pleasant experience. If there was a little more light, we could play some poker."

Fisher said grimly, "There's enough light and I've got a deck of cards in my pocket. We'll just play a few hands of heads-up poker and I'm going to have every cent that you have on you before dawn because I damn sure ain't going to sleep with that bundle of joy that you've got hid behind that boulder. How in the world could a man sleep never knowing if he's going to be blown to kingdom come without even being aware of it. Besides that, if I'm going to go out, I'm going to go out taking something of yours with me, namely your money."

Longarm said, "Well, Fish, there's no sense in you getting yourself worked up about it. I'm perfectly willing to play you some small-stakes heads-up poker. Get the cards out and spread a blanket around here so we can get some light on the subject. We ought to get some of that cheese and crackers out in case we want to break for a meal."

They played all through the night, dollar ante, five-dollar limit, five-card stud. By the first gray streaks of the false dawn, somewhere around five o'clock, Longarm had lost

215 dollars. It was all he had except the change in his pocket. He said, "Fish, I ain't got no money left. Will you take my marker?"

Fish gave him a look. "Is there a prospect of a gunfight?"

"I expect there is," Longarm said. "That's what we're here for."

"And you want me to take the marker of a man who is about to go into a gunfight?"

Longarm nodded his head gently. "You've got a point there, Fish. I don't know what's come over me lately. I guess I confused you with a human being."

"Tell you what I'll do," Fish said. "Since you are down, I'll allow you a hundred dollars on that dun horse of yours and we'll double the stakes."

Longarm said, "A hundred dollars for the dun? I paid three hundred dollars for that horse when he was a four-year-old. He's six now and he's worth two hundred dollars more than that now."

Fish said, "All right. I'll go a hundred and a half. Take it or leave it."

"Well, under the circumstances, I guess I'll have to take it, but let's triple the stakes. Three-dollar ante, fifteen-dollar limit."

"Oh, no, you don't. I didn't win your money with three dollars and fifteen dollars, and you ain't gonna win it back with three dollars and fifteen dollars. We'll double it, that's enough."

When true dawn finally broke some forty-five minutes later, Longarm had won all but fifty dollars of his money back. He said, slamming down his cards to indicate that was the last hand, "There, let that be a lesson to you, Fish. Don't ever loan anybody any money for a card game. You ought to know better than that."

106

"I can guarantee you that I will never again make that exception in your case. What now?"

Longarm yawned. "I guess we'd better get ready. I think we're going to have company coming. In fact, off yonder to the west I believe I hear the sound of the train that is supposed to bring the work crew to start in laying track."

Fish asked, "Then what's supposed to happen?"

"Then, if things go according to plan, I'm expecting the Gallagher bunch to come charging down on that track crew and wreck whatever work they've done. I don't know how long it will take them to get here. They may not arrive here before noon."

Fish said grimly, "In the meanwhile, it is going to start getting hot and that ice will begin to melt, and pretty soon that nitroglycerin is going to get right lively. Is that right, Mister Deputy Marshal Lawman Custis Long?"

"I ain't going to lie to you, Fish. That's a fact. They've brought a fresh supply of ice on that train that's bringing the workers in, and maybe you can slip down there and get us a batch of it in case we need some more. I just checked on the ice a few minutes ago and we've got half what we started with."

"Yeah, and it was damn near freezing last night."

In less than half an hour, the train came chugging out of the mountains, heading toward the end of the line. It was just an engine with a couple of flatbed cars behind it loaded with men and rails and cross-ties. Longarm shaded his eyes and tried his best to count the workers he could see. He said, "Looks like there is about twelve or fourteen of them."

Fish asked, "Are they supposed to be some help to us?"

"No. Their instructions are at the first sign of trouble, they are supposed to pile on that train and take off. The

107

engineer is supposed to keep the steam up."

"So, you're having them lay track to entice the Gallagher brothers in here. What makes you think the Gallagher brothers themselves will come?"

"Oh, I doubt very seriously that either one of the Gallagher brothers will be in the gang that attacks the tracklaying crew."

Fish asked, "Then what the hell are we doing here?"

Longarm looked at his friend. "Cutting down the odds, Fish, cutting down the odds. The real play, I feel, will take place this afternoon. The one thing that we have to try our best to do is to wipe out every man in this raiding party. I don't want a soul, if it can be helped, getting back to the strip or to Quitman and getting back to the Gallagher brothers. I assume you are still the shot you once were."

"I reckon that I can handle my end. That is, if that joy juice don't blow us into small pieces."

"Would you quit worrying about that nitro? It ain't blowed up yet."

Fish said, "And we won't know when it does. I suppose you're not worried."

"Of course I'm worried. I just don't see the point in talking about it all the time."

"I think you're scareder than I am."

"Dammit, Fish, shut up. Get ready. Get your weapons and your ammunition laid out. My God, we've got a fight coming up here, maybe. Try to act like you know what you're doing."

It was good daylight when the train crew and the workers dismounted. The workers went about their business preparing the roadbed to accept new cross-ties and then new rails. Longarm noticed that the engineer very carefully kept half-steam up in his boiler. Longarm could faintly hear the *chuf-chuf* of the engine, and he could see small white puffs of smoke and steam rising from the smokestack. The workers seemed to only have half their eye on their job. The other half was directed toward their east, where they expected the raiding party to appear. Longarm calculated that where he and Fish were positioned was about half a mile further east than where the workers were. If he didn't allow the bandits across a line drawn from the butte perpendicular to the line of the train, he didn't figure there was any danger to the workmen.

After a while he suggested that Fish go down and check on the horses. He said, "I don't figure there's any water around here, although that crew might have enough. Why don't you cinch them both up and ride over and see if you can get some water and any kind of feed that they might have. You might also see if you can fetch a fresh bag of ice."

Fish said, "I'm for that."

"Then I reckon when you bring the horses back into the grove of trees that you might leave them saddled and bridled."

"You mean in case we need to get out of here in a hurry?"

Longarm looked annoyed. "No. In case we have to give chase."

Fish said, "Oh, yeah. Nothing I'd like better than to give chase to about two dozen heavily armed bandits."

"Go on down, you skinny bastard, and see to those horses and make short work of it. It's getting on up into the day. It must be around seven-thirty now."

"I'm on my way."

While Fisher Lee was gone, Longarm carefully opened the tops of the canvas ice-filled sacks. He brushed away the top layer of the chopped ice. Halfway down in each one he found two ice-filled oilskin packets. With great care, he drew one out. It was dripping ice water. He opened the flap and looked inside. Nestled inside their private bed of crushed ice were two very innocent-looking small glass flasks full of clear white liquid. It was, he thought, a very nice arrangement that would allow him to take the nitro out a packet at a time, with two vials in each packet to use as needed.

He carefully replaced the oilskin packet back into the slit that the solidifying ice had created. The ice had not melted as much as he'd thought it would. It appeared to him that both sides were at least three-quarters full. He closed the sacks up and then looked at Pedro.

Longarm said to the burro, "Pedro, I'm sorry. I ain't got a thing for you. No water, no feed, no hay, nothing. Unless you want to eat rock, there's nothing."

The patient animal, who didn't seem to have moved an inch the entire night, looked at him with those big sad brown eyes and flicked an ear in recognition of Longarm's words.

Longarm said, "I wish most folks that I work with were as easy to work with as you are and as easy to please. Pedro, you're a credit to the U.S. marshals service."

He went back to the row of rocks along the edge of the ledge and looked as far as he could to the east. The terrain remained empty. In the still air, he could hear the men grunting and the scrape of the shovels as they prepared the roadbed in the rocky, sandy soil. Soon, they would start laying cross-ties, and after that would come the rails. He wondered what time the raiders would come.

In a few minutes, as he watched, he saw Fisher emerge from the top of the trees and head toward the train. It was amusing to see the workers look up, stare for a moment, drop their tools, and then carefully make their way quickly back to the engine. Even the engineer, who had been idling along the drive wheels, oiling this and that, immediately went up into the cab.

As Fisher neared waving his hat, they saw that it was just one man. Perhaps they had been told to expect some protection, perhaps they had not. At any rate, they seemed to receive Fisher without too much alarm. Longarm watched as Fisher dismounted and talked with the engineer and a member of the work crew who Longarm took to be the foreman. Finally, four men jumped up on one of the flat cars and wrestled down a big barrel. The way the horses crowded around, he could tell it was water. He didn't know if it was the men's water, but the horses didn't care. Unfortunately, there was no feed to be had, but after a while, one of the men came out of the coal tender lugging a canvas sack. He and Fisher arranged it over Longarm's saddle and then tied it in place. Longarm took it to be the extra ice he'd asked for.

After some more talk, Fisher wheeled and brought the horses back at a much slower pace. He disappeared from Longarm's view as he came around the back side of the butte. The one thing that had Longarm puzzled was that Fisher had somehow acquired a bucket of something heavy. He was carrying it in his right hand and reining with his left. Longarm assumed that sooner or later, Fisher would let him know. He also had a quiet smile to himself at the frustration of his friend when he, Longarm, had managed to win back most of his money. He'd even told Fisher, "Listen, if you sit there long enough, I'll not only have all my money back, but all of yours too."

Fisher had said, "There ain't no such day and there ain't never going to be such a day. You sit there long enough and I'll own everything you have including all the lies you've told about women."

111

It wasn't long before Longarm could hear grunts and scrambling noises from behind him. He figured it was Fisher losing more weight and having trouble with his slick-soled boots on the hard, rocky, angled sides of the butte. Then Fisher came into view, struggling along with the big bucket in his hand.

Longarm asked, "What do you have there? Some hot soup?"

Fisher was still out of breath, and it took him a moment before he could reply. "No, I've got some water for the only really necessary element of this organization, old Pedro."

Longarm smiled. "Now, that's damn thoughtful of you, Fisher. I'm really sorry that I've said the things that I've said about you around town."

Fisher said, "Go to hell." He took the water over to the grateful burro, who immediately plunged half his head into the bucket.

Longarm said, "Naturally, you didn't bring him any grain."

"Why . . ." Fisher stopped. "They didn't happen to have any grain, Mister Deputy Marshal Custis Long. They were not even aware of our presence. I did improvise on the spot, and I did try to get the horses fed. But I have them over in a better place than that little bit of woods and with some halfway decent grass. They're cinched up, but I took the bits out of their mouths so that they could graze. It shouldn't take us but a second or two to rebridle them."

"Well, I reckon that's all right. You done good, Fish, for a man of your capabilities."

Fisher kneeled down beside him and looked to his carbine. He said, "Any sign of anything?"

"No, nothing, just a lot of view. How did that train crew take to you coming up on them?"

112

Fish smiled. "Well, they were a mite apprehensive at first. I told them that we were just out here scouting the country for the surveyor."

"That was quick thinking. What did they say?"

"They warned me about the bandits."

"That was thoughtful of them."

"I didn't tell them there was already one up there on that butte, wearing a badge but a bandit just the same. I swear, Longarm, you cheated sometime in that card game. You had to have. There ain't no way you can beat me straight up."

"If anybody cheated, it was you. By the way, where is the ice that you brought from the train? That nitro is starting to sweat."

Fish jumped to his feet. "Oh, hell, I forgot it. It's down by the horses. I'm going after it now."

Longarm yelled after him, "Bring our canteens. It's getting warm up here and I don't know how long we are going to have to wait."

Fisher's voice came from around the curve on the trail. Longarm could hear him scrambling. Fish said, "Anything else?"

Longarm said, "Yeah, you might have remembered most of the stuff, but you didn't come back with nothing but a bucket of water for Pedro."

Longarm could hear the muffled sound of cursing. He laughed softly to himself.

The morning dragged on. They had very carefully added ice to the nitro, or rather, Longarm had added the ice. After one look, Fisher had retreated around to the other side of the butte, vowing that he didn't see any point in getting himself blown to pieces by a damn fool fooling around with something that he didn't know nothing about.

After that, they'd had a breakfast of cheese and saltines and canned peaches. It wasn't much, but as Fish had said, it was filling, especially the sardines.

They kept their eyes to the east. It got to be ten o'clock and then eleven. By then, the road crew had laid down fifty feet of cross-ties and were starting to bring up the rails. It was interesting to watch them. Four men with a kind of a tong instrument would each get ahold of a rail, lift it off the flatcar, pick it up again, and walk it up to its place atop the cross-ties. After that, two men, working in unison, would drive home the spikes that held it in place. The sledgehammer blows filled the valley with the constant sound of steel on steel.

Longarm said, "If they can't hear that, even in Quitman, then they're deaf. I have an idea that they keep a very close eye on this particular section of track."

Fisher said, "What about us? Maybe they've seen us and been spooked."

"We haven't showed ourselves since about eight o'clock, and they wouldn't be looking for us anyhow. They think they're the cock of the walk around here. They'll come unless they plan to let Mister Simmons get his railroad built, which I seriously doubt since they don't quite have as much money in their headquarters in Springer as they would like."

Fisher said testily, "Well, dammit, I wish they would come. I'm getting tired of this."

Longarm said, "Get out the cards. You still have about fifty dollars of my money."

Fisher reached in his pocket. "Get over here close. We'll play under the lee of these rocks where there is at least a little shade. I can tell you this one thing. Once I win all your money, I ain't loaning you no more, not even on that damn plug horse of yours."

114

It was just after noon when Fisher raised his head. He said, "I think I hear something."

Longarm said, "Probably pounding in your ears because you are getting your ass whipped here." Longarm had won all of his money back and about fifty dollars of Fisher's.

Fisher said, "No, be quiet. I'm serious. I have real sensitive hearing and I think I can hear something."

Longarm sat still, his ear cocked. Before long he too could hear the distant sound of hoofbeats. In the desert, sound carried a long way. He said to Fisher, "Take your hat off and peek over that rock and see if you see any dust."

Very cautiously, Fisher raised up until his eyes were just above the level of the boulders. He said, "I can kind of see a faint haze, but I ain't real sure. Let's give it a few minutes more."

Longarm said, "If it's them, I think you better understand the situation. What do you think it is down there to the valley? About two hundred yards?"

"Two fifty, three hundred yards. It's a pretty good rifle shot, if that's what you're getting at."

"If plans go the way I want them to, you'll be doing most of the shooting. Use my rifle and yours. If I can, I'll try to reload for you. But the idea is to stop them. If you can't hit men, shoot horses. We'll deal with them on foot later on. I don't want them getting any closer to that train crew than five or six hundred yards."

Fisher smiled. "As skittish as that train crew is, I think they'll be gone long before we fire the first shots. At the first sign of the bandits, they're going to have that engine backing up at thirty miles an hour."

Five minutes passed. Fisher said, "Yeah, I see dust. It's a pretty good cloud, too, Longarm. Must be at least a dozen horses, maybe more. Of course, all I can see right now is dust."

They waited. Cautiously, Longarm turned to his left and crawled to the end of the last boulder that they were using for protection. He took off his hat and peered around the corner. Just as his eyes focused off in the distance, he could see between two big buttes, one mounded and one jagged, a little rise. As he watched, he could see the dust cloud top the rise and come into view. The riders were perhaps two miles off.

As they neared, individual figures of men and horses began to appear. Longarm said, "A dozen, hell. Looks closer to two dozen to me."

Chapter 7

When the riders were about a little over a mile away, Fisher said, "I make it an even eighteen."

Longarm said, "Oh, hell, Fish. You can't see that good so that you can count that many men in a bunch."

Fisher said evenly, "If I couldn't see that good, Longarm, I wouldn't still be alive."

Longarm stared at the approaching gang of bandits. "Well, you got me beat. I can see them pretty clearly, but I can't pick them out. What color is the hat of the man in front?"

Fisher said, "It's a light tan, a little dusty around the hat band."

Longarm looked to his right. He could hear the engine begin to *chug* and could see the crew scrambling back toward it. "Looks like our crew from the railroad ain't going to stand around and watch the fun." He paused thoughtfully for a second. "I wonder who it is from the Silverado outfit in Springer that gets word to the Gallaghers in Quitman when the train crew is going out?"

Fisher's head swiveled around and he looked at Longarm. He asked, "You reckon that's how they know?"

"Can you think of any other way?"

Fisher shook his head. "Well, I'll be dogged. I do believe that you're right. That's the only way. How do you reckon your Mister Simmons is going to figure out who the traitor is?"

Longarm said with a thin smile on his face, "If things go the way I hope they do, he won't have to. Now, I reckon we'd better get back to work." He got up and went over to the canvas sacks, carefully lifted up one flap, and with equal care carefully brushed the ice away from two of the oilskin envelopes that contained two of the nitroglycerin vials each. As gently as he could, he lifted them out of their nests and started back toward his place behind the rock. As he neared, he could see that Fisher was staring at him in horror.

He asked, "What's the matter with you, Fisher? Ain't you ever seen a man carrying nitroglycerin before?"

Fisher's voice trembled. "My, God. What are you going to do with that stuff? I can't believe that you're going to bring it right over next to us."

Longarm knelt down, carefully setting the oilskin packets on the ground in the shade of the rocks. With careful fingers, he lifted the flap of one of the packets, exposing the two glass vials still nestled in the remaining bed of ice.

Fisher had taken an involuntary step or two backwards. He said, "Sonofabitch! You got that stuff right here! What are you going to do?"

Longarm glanced up, easing his face around the rock until he could see the horsemen. "I make them to be about three quarters of a mile off. What do you reckon? And by the way, it looks like eighteen to me also."

Fisher said, "Yeah, I guess so, but right now I am considerably more concerned with what you're doing with that

118

dynamite juice. Longarm, do you have any idea how dangerous that stuff is? What are you going to do with it?"

For answer, Longarm reached into his saddlebags and pulled out the slingshot he'd had made. He held it by the wooden handle and put his finger in the leather pouch and tested the rubber cords, stretching it out to see how springy it was. To his right, Fisher gasped.

Fisher said, "I hope you're not fixing to do what I think you're fixing to do."

Longarm looked around at him. "What? Did you think I was going to throw those damn vials?"

Fisher had gone white under his tan. He said in a trembling voice, "Longarm, you can't do this. Look here, you're going to draw that slingshot back. What if one of them rubber bands busts? The jolt will set one of them sonofabitches off and blow you and me right off this butte."

Longarm said matter-of-factly, "Yes, that could happen."

Fisher said, "Or when you release that thing, after you've drawn it back and then catapulted it out there, hell, the motion alone is going to shake it up. Longarm, this ain't going to work. My God, man, this ain't going to work."

Longarm said, "I'm counting on them being so cold that it'll take a considerable shock like hitting the ground to make the stuff blow up."

"You're counting on it? You mean you're guessing."

"Well, sometimes a man has to do a little guessing in life."

"Not with my life, he don't."

"Fisher, take it easy. This is safe. Ain't you ever taken a chance before?"

"This ain't a chance, Longarm. You ain't taking a chance. You are working your way right close to getting

119

us blown all to hell. Have you lost your mind?"

"You're making too much out of this thing, Fisher." He said it with conviction, but his own hands were trembling slightly as he fiddled with the slingshot. "How far off do you reckon they are now?"

Fisher lifted a cautious eye over the rock. "They're coming now pretty quick. They're in a gallop. I think they're going to try and get off a few shots at the crew. That engine is getting off mighty slow. I don't think they left enough steam in the boiler. That train crew better get to hustling or they're going to get a few holes in their smokestack."

Longarm said, "Not if this stuff works like I think it will work. Tell me where they are now."

Fisher said, "They're about two hundred yards to our left coming straight down the middle between the buttes and heading straight for the engine. They've got their horses at a hard run now. A few of them have their pistols drawn, a few of them have rifles out."

Longarm said, "I reckon it's time then." Willing his hand to be steady, he reached out and plucked one of the delicate glass vials from its icy nest. As gently as he could, he put it into the leather pouch of the slingshot, holding it delicately but firmly with the thumb and forefinger of his right hand. He held the handle of the slingshot and said tensely to Fisher, "Where are they now?"

Fisher said in a faint voice, "These may be the last words I speak, but they are nearly even with us now. If you're going to let that thing off, you'd better do it pretty quick."

Longarm rose to a half-crouch, enough to see the band of men as they were starting to pass the butte. He let them pass it by it about fifty yards and then with a prayer in his heart, pulled back the pouch of the slingshot as far as the rubber would stretch. Then, with as gentle a motion as he could, he released it. The glass vial flew through the Y of the slingshot and arced through the air. Both Fisher and Longarm watched in fascination as the vial arced further and further out and as the horsemen rode closer to its eventual descent.

The two men lost sight of it as it fell toward the ground, but then, an instant later, there came a terrific explosion right in front of the charging gang of bandits. A cloud of smoke and dust and dirt went up. They could see a flash of fire at its center. Following the thunderclap of an explosion, they could hear the high whinnies of the horses and the shouts and curses of men. Longarm had only a moment to survey what he had done. Then he knelt and took the second vial out of the oilskin pouch, carefully put it in the leather pouch of the slingshot, aimed it toward the middle of the bunch, and fired it, arcing it high in the air, watching it tumble end over end and then start down, down, toward the band that was intent on destroying the railroad. Only then could he see that several horses were down and a like number of men. Beside him, Fisher Lee was methodically firing his rifle. Longarm saw men fall out of the saddle suddenly. He saw horses go down suddenly. He was aware that Fisher had changed guns and that he was now firing Longarm's carbine.

Then the second vial hit, exploding even louder than the first. This time, it hit right in the middle of the bandits. There was the same flash of fire, then smoke and a high-rising cloud of dirt and dust.

Fisher said, "My God. Would you look at that?"

Longarm said, "Keep shooting, dammit."

As swiftly as he could and as carefully as he could, Longarm knelt and took another vial from the second pouch and fired it into the air. He was aiming this time behind the milling, frightened, scattering riders. He didn't take time to watch this one land. Without pause, he bent to get the forth vial of the nitro. This time, he fired in a flatter arc, aiming to hit beyond the crowd of men who were by now so obscured by smoke and confusion that it was difficult to tell how many were down and how many were still up and riding. Even Fisher was now spacing his shots.

With the boom of the fourth explosion sounding in his ears, Longarm stepped quickly to the big sacks of ice and took out the third oilskin packet. As quickly as he could, he returned to his firing place, lifted out one of the vials, placed it in the slot of the slingshot, and fired, watching the twinkling glass oblong as it sparkled in the sun. He was already leaning down to reach for the sixth vial when he heard the explosion. This time, he fired without looking. There wasn't much point. The smoke and dust made it nearly impossible to tell what the situation was below.

To his right, Fisher said in an anxious voice, "Ain't you done yet? You've set off six of those damn things and I can't see a damn thing that I'm shooting at."

"Yeah, I think I'll save the other two. I might have a use for one or two of them later."

Fisher said, "I ain't riding a foot further with you and those damn things. My God, will that dust never settle?"

He suddenly sighted and fired as a man broke out of the smoky haze. The shot knocked the horse down and the man went sprawling. He landed on his knees and started running toward the unfinished track. Fisher followed him with his rifle and fired. The bullet kicked dust up in front of the man. He wheeled as Fisher levered another shell into his carbine and then, aiming carefully, fired again. The man threw up his arms and pitched over backwards.

Longarm took up his own rifle and reached into his pocket where he kept some spare cartridges. As fast as he could, he rammed them home into his rifle. Then he leaned across the rock just in front of him, watching the back of the mass of smoke and confusion. Two riders suddenly burst out, heading back in the direction that they had come. He shot the first, leading him slightly, knocking him out of the saddle. The shot caused the second man to veer off to the right, taking him rapidly out of range as Longarm levered another shell into the chamber. He fired, knowing it was a chance shot and knowing that he would have to be lucky. He aimed for the man's thigh, hoping that if he missed the man, it would hit the horse. The bullet went harmlessly wild and the man galloped on. Longarm hollered loud, "Fisher, quick, this way."

They both swung their rifles in unison at the fleeing rider. They fired at the same time, and for a second it seemed that they had missed. Then the rider slumped forward in his saddle as the horse stumbled. The horse went head-down, flipping over on his back. The rider fell with him. After a second, the horse scrambled to his feet and ran off, trailing his reins. The rider lay in a crumpled heap.

Now, some of the smoke was starting to clear, some of the haze and some of the dust. What they saw was hard to believe. Some twelve horses were down and at least that many men. Longarm took a quick count. At best, he saw four riders, still aimlessly trying to find their way. Together, he and Fisher methodically concentrated on first one and then the other, firing simultaneously at the man the closest to his escape route. Within two minutes, all four were down.

It was suddenly all over. The only sound down below was a scream of wounded horses and the faint moans of a few men. Here and there, riderless horses ran backwards and forward, confused by the noise and the disturbance. It was quiet only in the sense that the earth-shattering explosions no longer sounded.

Fisher said, almost in awe, "Would you look at them holes in the ground down there, Longarm. This looks like what I would imagine war would look like."

Longarm said, "I guess we'd better get down there. Did you see anyone get away?"

Fisher shook his head. "No, the only thing that I can think of is that somebody rode south and we wouldn't have been able to see them through the dust and smoke that those bombs of yours was throwing up, but nobody came this way, nobody went north, and nobody went east, so it had to have been south."

Longarm said, "Let's go down and take a count. I sure as hell hope you were right about there being eighteen in that party. I sure as hell can't take the chance and let one of them break away and get back to the Gallagher brothers."

Fisher said, "How do you know that one of them ain't a Gallagher or maybe both of the brothers? How do you know that?"

Longarm said, "I told you before. The Gallaghers don't do their own dirty work. That's how they have lasted as long as they have. We better get on down there."

Fisher said, "Some of the men are wounded, but that don't mean they can't shoot. You don't have to be that strong to shoot."

"You come at them from one end and I'll come at them from the other. We'll stay well out of pistol range and we'll let them know what will happen if a gun gets fired."

"All right, Boss, then let's go."

"Did you just call me Boss?"

124

"Longarm, I'm going to call anybody Boss that can create as much destruction as you just did with that slingshot and those bottles of clear hell."

With an effort, they scrambled their way down off the butte carrying their carbines and their freshly reloaded revolvers. Longarm led the way to the grove of trees where their horses were tied and pulled up the cinch, put the bit back into his horse's mouth, and mounted. When Fisher was ready, they rode slowly toward the scene of carnage some quarter of a mile away.

Longarm said, "You go on to the west there and I'll go off to the east. Stay at least one hundred yards away from the nearest man. I'm going to call out to them and see if they have any sense. If one of them fires, don't hesitate."

"You can make money betting that I will do that."

As they approached the men and the horses that lay in jumbled heaps and piles, they separated, Fisher going toward the railhead end and Longarm riding off toward the direction from which the bandits had first appeared. Now and then, Longarm could see a man raise his head and watch him. Once, one of them waved a white handkerchief. He didn't wave it long. After a moment, his arm fell limply to his side.

When he considered himself in position, Longarm called out, "I'm Deputy Marshal Custis Long of the U.S. marshals service. You men are all under arrest. Now, there is another lawman on the opposite side from me. If one of you so much as looks like you want to fire a gun, he's going to shoot you and I'm going to do the same. There are wounded among you and we'd like to get you some help, but if you give us the least resistance, you're going to get a bullet. Depend on it. If you have any guns near you, I'm telling you right now, sling them as far away from you as you can. All they are is a death warrant. I'm going to give you one minute by my watch to get yourself disarmed. Then we will start amongst you. I promise you that you will not gain a thing by being brave or revengeful. We are holding all the cards."

With that, Longarm dismounted and dropped the reins of his horse. The dun would ground-rein and would stand in that position so long as his reins were touching the ground. Longarm cocked the hammer of his Winchester and started forward with the gun at the ready. Across the way, he could see Fisher doing the same. Wounded horses were still neighing and screaming.

Longarm said, "Anybody that is wounded, hold up your hand if you can. If you can't, make a sound of some kind."

As he watched, four hands went up and he heard a couple of whimpers. He slowly moved through the men from the eastern side, and Fisher came from the west. It was an ugly sight. Horses and mounts were ripped apart in some cases. Others were simply shot. Now and again, he saw a man with an entire limb missing. It was as gory a sight as he believed he had ever seen in his long years of law enforcement.

Longarm said. "All right, are there any among you that can walk or crawl? If so, I want you to crawl toward the west toward those tracks. I want you to do it now."

As he watched, three men, two of them crawling and one of them limping, made their way toward Fisher. Longarm said, "When you get clear of this bunch, I want you to lay down face flat on the ground with your legs spread and your arms extended."

Fisher said, "I've got to start killing these wounded horses. I can't stand listening to them much longer."

"All right, you do it. I'll stand watch over the men."

Methodically, one by one, Fisher moved among the wounded animals, shooting each one squarely in the head. Little by little, the distressing noise from the animals subsided.

Longarm was about to take a step further into the midst of the men when he saw a man who appeared dead, lying on his stomach, slowly work a revolver out from under his chest, sighting on Fisher. Without pause, Longarm flung the carbine to his shoulder, aimed at the back of the man's head, which was only fifteen yards off, and then fired. There was a loud *thunk* and the man heaved up in the air and then fell flat.

Furiously, Longarm yelled at them, "That sound you just heard was the sound of a fool getting shot. Any more of you want to be heroes? I'll drag the next one of you sonofabitches that tries that behind my horse for ten miles before I shoot him."

Finally, all the dead were counted and all the wounded had been either helped or carried clear of the rest. There were eighteen raiders in all, five wounded and thirteen dead.

Off in the distance, Longarm could barely see the head of the engine of the train half hidden from view behind a butte. He could see puffs of smoke rising from the stack. He said to his friend, "Fish, we've got to get these men some help. They need to be carried into Springer where they can see a doctor. Why don't you ride on over there and tell the engineer to bring the train up. Then get some of the workmen to load these wounded men onto those flatcars and bring them back into Springer."

It took a long half hour for Fisher to ride to the train, for the engineer to bring his two flatbed cars up to the end of the rails, and for the workmen to get down and carry the wounded men back to the train. Longarm looked at his watch anxiously. It was after one in the afternoon, and he and Fisher were at least ten miles from the Oklahoma border where they were supposed to meet the Gallagher brothers. As far as he was concerned, the meeting was still on, and as far as he was concerned, that meeting was the cause of the slaughter that had just taken place.

When the wounded were taken aboard and the train was about ready to pull out, Longarm rode over and signaled to the engineer to come to him. He had decided on the engineer as the best man to be trusted with his suspicions. He told the engineer what he thought: that somewhere in the camp of the Silverado Mining Company was a spy for the Gallaghers who rode out and notified them whenever there was to be work done on the track. The engineer scratched his head and looked surprised.

Then the engineer said, "You know, that makes a hell of a lot of sense. Every time we've tried to work this last month, no matter what day we tried to work or what hour, no matter how many days we skipped, they'd always come down on us about four-five hours after we got cranked up."

"In other words, about the amount of time it would take to ride from the headquarters into Quitman and then from Quitman to here."

The engineer nodded. "I see what you're saying, neighbor."

"If I was you, I wouldn't speak of it to anyone else except Eugene and ask him to tell Mister Simmons. But I think it's very likely that you have a spy in your midst. What I would do is schedule a work party, and then I would see who came up sick or lame the next morning or who left camp and was suddenly missing or who couldn't go along. You may not have that trouble anymore. It might be settled."

128

The engineer looked at all the dead men lying out on the prairie. He said, "Yeah, but their kind is a dime a dozen. From what I've heard of the Gallaghers, they can raise fifty more of them overnight. No, I don't reckon this business is finished, but I'll sure keep it under my hat, this tip you gave me. I'm much obliged to you, Marshal."

Longarm asked the engineer if he would wait, saying that he had another passenger for him. Without telling Fisher where he was going, he spurred his horse over to the foot of the butte, and then clambered up to the rocky ledge where they had made their fight. He had two vials of the nitro left, but he wouldn't be able to take Pedro with him, not on the ride that they were going to have to make to the territorial line between Oklahoma and New Mexico. Nevertheless, he was going to use the burro to carry the iced nitro back down the butte.

With great care, Longarm loaded the canvas sacks back on the burro and secured them in place with ropes, and then took Pedro's lead rope and started down the craggy half-mountain, half-rock. It was with some relief that he finally reached the bottom. He mounted his horse, taking Pedro on lead, and rode slowly over to the train.

He could see Fisher watching him. Of course, Fisher didn't know there was another oilskin packet remaining in the canvas sacks. Longarm did.

At the train, he dismounted and carefully took the canvas bags off the burro. He patted the animal affectionately, and then saw that two of the crewmen lifted the burro up onto the flatcar. He said, "Take care of my old buddy there. He's earned his keep today. Somebody make sure that he gets fed."

One of the workmen said, "Oh, you don't need to worry about that, sir. This here burro is one of Mister

Eugene's favorites. He'll give him a mighty good feed tonight."

Fisher and Longarm stood and watched as the train slowly backed down the line. In five minutes, it was out of sight back behind the next butte. After that, Longarm began the tender process of packing the two vials separately in each of his saddlebags. He gave all of his ammunition and his extra revolver to Fisher along with the remaining bottle of whiskey that he had.

Fisher said, "You ain't going to do what I think you're going to do, are you?"

"I don't have much choice, Fish."

"Well, I can tell you somebody who is not going to ride beside you."

"I don't blame you. If I's you, I'd ride half a mile away."

"Yeah, sure, so you could say that I was scared. You'd like that, wouldn't you?"

"No, I'd much rather have your company, to tell you the truth."

Fisher gave him an astonished look. "Why, you sonofabitch. You don't care much about a friend if you'd just as soon see him get blown sky-high with you."

Longarm was busy packing his saddlebags with ice. He had brought one of the empty oilskin pouches with him. He loaded it with ice before carefully putting one of the vials of nitro inside, then closed the flap and buried it in the ice already in his saddlebags. That left the second vial by itself. He reloaded its contents with ice and put it in the other side of the saddlebags.

Fisher stood there in stunned silence, watching him. "I hope you realize that it ain't exactly the same as that burro carrying them. That horse of yours is way and gone more jouncy than that burro."

Longarm put his foot in his stirrup and stepped aboard his horse. He said, "I ain't got a choice, Fisher." He had the slingshot in his hand and he turned, unbuckled the flap of his saddlebags, and put it in with one of the vials of nitro.

Fisher said, "What in hell makes you think that you're going to need that?"

"I still think that we'll be badly outnumbered, or at least I'll be badly outnumbered. You'll be coming back this way. I think I've got a bad need for that nitro."

Fisher said, "I think that you've got a bad need for somebody to cut a hole in your head and look inside and see what's in there. I think there's a whole bunch of crazy people running around in there."

Longarm said, "Fish, we've got to get moving. We're late right now."

As they set off eastward at what Fisher declared was too fast a pace, although in reality it was nothing more than a steady walk, Longarm fretted about the time and the distance to the line. He said, "Fish, this is the best chance that I've ever had in my life to get the worst men that I've ever known. I can't mess this one up. This one has got to happen."

"Well, hell. Looks like we made a pretty good start on them back yonder."

Longarm said, "Yeah, but it's like what the engineer done took note of: Those were two-bit gunhands. The Gallaghers can get fifty more with just a wave of their hand. We didn't do more than cut down on the force at hand. I'm going to bet that they have anywhere from half a dozen to a dozen back with them in Quitman."

Fisher shook his head. "You wouldn't think there was that many bad folks in this world, would you?"

"Well, you were a lawman, Fisher. You should know."

131

Fisher said, "It's the times, Longarm. When times are hard, everybody turns to crime. They don't think there is any other way of getting any money, so they turn to pointing pistols at other people. I blame the government for this."

Longarm gave him a look. "That's like blaming the bull that fathered the calf that grew up to be a steer that you ate a steak off that was too tough. That don't make a bit of sense. A man can make his own way, he don't need no outside help."

"Spoken like a man who gets his meals at the federal trough."

Longarm smiled thinly. "What are you doing way over there, Fisher? I'm getting tired of raising my voice talking to you. Why don't you ride up closer?"

Fisher said, "I'm just fine right where I am."

Longarm chuckled. "Do you think that twenty-yard separation's going to make any difference to this nitro? It's going to blow you just as high as it's going to blow me, if it goes off."

"Longarm, don't be turning your head toward me. You look straight ahead for gopher holes or anything else that your horse might stumble over. You better handle that animal better than anything you've ever handled in your life."

"Fisher, if you'd have caught a stray bullet while we were up on that butte, would you have been any less dead than you would have been if you'd been blown up by this nitro?"

"The point is, I didn't get hit by no stray bullet, and yet here I am, a damn fool, riding alongside of a man that has enough explosives on the ass end of his horse to make us as flat as this prairie."

"I think we're going to have to strike a trot to get there in time."

132

"You just strike all the trots you want to, but you give me fair warning when you do so I can get the hell out of here."

Longarm laughed slightly. "No, I'm serious, Fisher. What I think that you better do is to lope on ahead and see if you can spot them. If you do, get word to them that I am coming but my horse is lame and I'm having to take it slow."

Fisher smiled. "You know, I think that's the best idea that I've heard you have in my life. You keep on thinking like that and you'll never get any argument out of me. Are you serious?"

"It appears to me that we're going to be about half an hour late. I calculate it's still four or five miles to the border and it's after two and at the pace we're going, we're not going to make it. Why don't you gallop on up there and see if you can keep the situation in hand."

"I can promise you that I am more than willing. Do you want me to bring the other brother back—Rufus, the one with the scar on his jaw?"

"I doubt that he would come until they got me. I wouldn't get too close to them, Fisher. Just keep within shooting distance and let them know what is happening, let them know that I will be along in no less than half an hour. Don't go up there and get yourself taken prisoner, do you understand me? If they act hostile, get your ass out of there."

"Longarm, you're still talking sensible. I think there may be hope for you yet."

"There's one other thing that we need to get settled before we come up on them. Let's assume that everything goes smooth and Rufus comes on this side with you and I go off with Clem. As soon as you get out of sight of us, I want you to take care of Rufus."

133

"Do you mean kill him?"

"Not unless you have to. I'll leave that to your own judgment, but as quick as you can, I want you to get the drop on him and knock him on the head and tie him up. Do something so he will stay where you leave him. As soon as you are finished with him, I want you to come toward where I am and kind of scout around."

Fisher gave him a sly look. "So it turns out that you figure that you might need my help. Is that correct, Mister Deputy Marshal Custis Long?"

"Yes, Fisher. I am reduced to such a level that I might even need your help. I hate to admit it, but that's the case. I don't know what I'm going to run into. But if you do see that I am in big trouble, don't try and get me out of it by yourself. Go for help, do you understand? Wire Billy Vail at Denver and get every damn marshal you can to get me loose from whatever bear trap they got me in."

"That part I think I can handle."

"Well, that's it then. You better get to kicking."

"My friend, that's something I can do." With that, Fisher put spurs to his horse and started off in a high lope, heading east to the Oklahoma border.

As his friend grew smaller in the distance with every passing moment, Longarm realized that he had never felt more lonely in his life. The two ounces of clear liquid trailing along right behind him were no comfort at all.

Chapter 8

He made better time than he previously thought he would. By three-thirty, he could see several figures in the distance. He assumed they were somewhere around the line between the two territories. It had become brutally hot, and Longarm was aware of just how fast the extra ice that he stuffed into his saddlebags was melting and leaking out. He hoped that the ice that was packed in the oilskin packets was faring much better. He could look back and see how the water had stained the leather of his saddlebags. Of course, it wouldn't do to ride up to the Gallagher brothers with water dripping out of his saddlebags.

The figures were coming near enough now, but he could see one much closer. As he watched, the man raised his arm and he could tell that it was Fisher Lee. Some two hundred yards past Fish, two other men sat on their horses. Longarm could only get an indistinct impression of them through the shimmering heat waves that rose from the desert plains. He noticed, about a mile further on, some kind of structure sitting out in the middle of nowhere. He couldn't tell if it was a house or a barn or some sort of warehouse. At the moment, he wasn't concerned. His only concern was making sure one of the Gallaghers went with Fisher while the other Gallagher brother stayed with *him*.

As he neared, Longarm saw Fish turn his horse and lope toward him. In a few moments, his tall, lanky friend was near enough to speak. Fisher said, "Well, I see you've made it this far."

Longarm said, "Better keep your voice down. What did you tell them?"

"I told them that your horse was lame. I told him that I thought that he had bowed a tendon and that you'd be here if you had to carry the horse."

"How close did you get to them?"

"Very damn unclose."

"Were you able to tell if one of them had a very long white scar along his jaw?"

Fisher said, "Kind of. It looked like it, but then again, I just told them I would hold my ground until you arrived. Naturally, they invited me to come on over for a parley, but I chose to tell them that it was my bound duty to keep an eye out for you."

"Do they still seem agreeable to the terms?"

"Yeah, as far as I can tell." Fisher was looking at Longarm's saddlebags. "Marshal, I don't know if you know it or not, but your saddlebags is kind of a dead giveaway that you're carrying something in there that most folks don't normally carry."

Longarm said, "I'm going to pull my horse up and I'm going to dismount. While I am looking like I'm busy getting some kind of ointment out of them, in reality I am going to be emptying some of the extra ice. I want you to take a look at my horse's front leg and pretend that it really was a bowed tendon."

Fisher said, "You want me to get off this horse and stand by your horse while you go to fooling around with the nitroglycerin that's in your saddlebags. Is that correct?"

"Yes."

Fisher sighed and dismounted. "I'm going to a doctor when I get back. There is something seriously wrong with a man who would do things like this, especially for the money. Do you realize that you have some of my money from that poker game? That wasn't supposed to happen, Longarm."

"If I ever get you to sit still long enough, I'll own all your money and your soul and what little brains you have."

They both dismounted, and while Longarm cleared out the last of the ice that was not contained in the oilskin packets, Fisher made busywork out of looking at Longarm's horse's front legs. Longarm took a peek inside each oilskin pouch. The situation in them was much better. There was still a pound of ice in each packet and if they did melt, the oilskin bags were watertight and nothing would spill out. Nonetheless, the sun was getting hotter, and it wouldn't be too much longer before the nitro would become more of a hazard to the man carrying it than to anyone it might be aimed at.

Longarm buckled the flaps of his saddlebags and remounted. He said, "Well, let's go ahead and get this over with. It doesn't look like more than half a mile. You ride on out wide ahead of me so that we don't make too inviting of a target. Don't take your carbine out, but have your hand on it. If they do anything funny, take a shot."

Fisher said, "Why in hell don't we shoot them now?"

Longarm said, "Because I am not sure it's the two Gallaghers. It would be like them to send two substitutes in their place to see what we are going to do. It wouldn't mean a damn thing to them if we shot a couple more of their men. No, there's no use in showing any more of our hand until we are sure that we have the goods. The only way that we can make sure is to find the one with the big scar on his jaw."

Fisher said, "Yeah, according to your girlfriend. I wonder how many men can call her their girlfriend?"

"That ain't the point, Fisher. I just don't think she is smart enough to lie to me."

"Longarm, when it comes to you and women, hell, you'll believe anything if it gets you between their legs."

"That's a hell of a thing to say to a man, especially one of my taste and discrimination."

"You're discriminating, all right, and you have taste, all right, although most of it is in your mouth. I'd say that you discriminate. If she's a woman, she's got to have a pulse."

Ahead they could see the two men separate a little as Longarm and Fisher approached. Longarm said, "Seems like they have the same idea that we do. Let's pull up to within a hundred yards of them and talk terms and how exactly we are going to do this."

Fisher said, "Sounds to me like somebody has to trust somebody, and I don't think they're the trusting kind. I damn sure don't feel like being trusting to folks such as them."

Longarm said, "Let's just see how it goes. At least they're here."

"Yeah, if it's them."

As they rode forward, the other pair of men started in their direction. They came fifty yards farther as Longarm and Fisher slowly advanced. With the distance down to about fifty or seventy-five yards, both sides pulled up. Longarm could not quite make out the features of either man, but he could see the white scar along the jaw of the man to his left. He stood up in his stirrups and yelled, "Gallagher? You be the Gallaghers?"

The one on the right said, "Yeah, are you Marshal Custis Long, the one they call Longarm?"

"That's correct. I hear you want to talk to me. I hear you have some wrongdoers that you want to deliver into my custody. Is that correct?"

The one doing the talking said, "Well, that's right as far as that goes, but that don't cover the whole business of the matter. I'm willing to turn these men over to you if you'll give us a fair ear as to how come we're being hounded and run down and persecuted like we've been when me and my brother ain't never done nothing wrong."

Longarm asked, "Who am I talking to?"

"Hell, you're talking to Clem Gallagher. Who did you think that you were talking to?"

"Who's the other man?"

"That's my brother, Rufus. Hell, don't you recognize him? I thought you had seen both of us. God knows, you've deviled us long enough. I thought you'd know us both by sight."

Longarm said, "No, just from a distance and mostly from the back."

"Yeah, I reckon that my shoulder blades twitched a little bit. Must have been just out of range."

"The last man I shot in the back just happened to turn at the wrong moment."

Clem Gallagher said, "I'll make damn sure that I don't make that mistake."

Longarm said, "All right. How do you want to do it? I'm not coming over there until you give me somebody over here. Is Rufus willing to come over here? This is Fisher Lee. He's a deputy U.S. Marshal out of the Santa Fe office."

Clem Gallagher said, "I thought them were the terms, although I didn't know you all had an office in Santa Fe."

"It was my understanding that you didn't get around the New Mexico territory very much, you didn't care for it, and you didn't have that many kinfolk there."

"I'm willing to go through with the agreement that we made through Lily Gail."

Longarm said, "All right. Send Rufus over. As soon as he crosses over, I'll cross over to you. By the way, what is that shack over there?"

Clem Gallagher turned in his saddle and looked back in the direction of the old building. He said, "Oh, just some old sodbuster that didn't make it. He tried to make a living growing rocks and cactus. I guess he thought that corn would grow in sand. It's just a big old falling-down house."

Longarm said, "Where are these men that you plan to deliver to me?"

Clem said, "They are right handy. If we reach an agreement, I can promise you that no less than fourteen men will be turned over to you, maybe more."

"How come your brother never says anything?"

"He ain't the talking kind."

"Start him forward and I'll start at the same time."

Longarm watched the other man as, for a moment, he talked to Clem Gallagher. The scar was plain as he worked his mouth.

Clem Gallagher yelled, "Rufus wants to make it damn clear that he's not going to surrender his weapon."

"I don't expect him to. Neither will I surrender mine. However, Clem, if anybody else joins us, then you're going to surrender yours."

Clem said, "It's just me and you, Marshal. Dammit, I told you that all I want to do is talk. How come you can't believe an honest man?"

"I do believe honest men. Start your brother."

Clem Gallagher nodded at the man beside him, and suddenly the man with the silver scar on his jaw started his horse toward Fisher. Longarm touched the spurs to the flanks of his dun and matched Rufus, if in fact that was who he was, stride for stride as they neared the invisible boundary between them.

Off to his left, Fisher said, "Good luck, Longarm. I hope you don't need any."

Without taking his eyes off either man, Longarm said, "Unlike some card players I know, I don't depend on luck, Fisher. You'd better mind yourself."

Fisher said, "I believe I can hold up my end."

"Well, we ought to get this over with pretty quick."

Then, off to his left, the man called Rufus passed across the invisible line at the same time Longarm did. Longarm touched his horse again lightly with his spurs so that he increased to a faster walk. Then, suddenly remembering he was supposed to be riding a crippled animal, he quickly slowed him again.

As he neared, Clem Gallagher said, "Is he stove up bad?"

"No. He got a loose shoe at the wrong time. I think it pulled his tendon a little bit. I nailed the shoe back tight. He seems to be improving considerable, but I don't want to stretch him. I'm a long way from home and I just as soon he not go lame out here."

They slowly came together and for the first time in all the years that he had been hunting them, Longarm was face to face with one of the Gallagher brothers.

The man had on a black, flat-crowned, straight-brimmed hat of good quality. He had on a white linen duster that reached to his knees. Under it, Longarm could see that he was wearing a good-quality shirt and corduroy pants. Longarm could just see the hammer and the back of the handle of what he took to be a Colt .44 with horn grips. Gallagher's face was small and mean and pinched-looking. His eyes appeared to Longarm to be just a trifle too close together. His lips were thin and he had almost no chin. He had the look that Longarm had seen before in men who were just a little too mean, too greedy, and too vicious for their own good and for the good of those who chanced to cross their path.

Longarm was surprised at the age of the man. Even with the pencil-thin mustache that decorated his lip, he couldn't have been more than thirty, if that. Longarm noticed that he had small hands. His face was not as weathered as it should have been for a man who spent time in the open. Longarm figured that the Gallagher style was to make the plans and then send others out to do the dirty work. Probably some of the men that had been enticed into the morning attack had been just that kind, but then, they were replaceable.

Longarm could not quite figure Gallagher's size in the saddle, but he doubted that he would be very big. At the most, he would be five-seven or five-eight and weigh around 140 pounds. Longarm hoped that he would get the chance to put his fist through that smug, selfish little face that was trying to lure him into a trap. Longarm was in no hurry, but he was looking forward to telling Clem Gallagher at the right moment what had happened to eighteen of his riders and why he wouldn't be tearing up anymore railroad lines and why he wasn't going to be robbing the mining office in Springer.

But all that could wait. Longarm wanted to look the situation over very carefully before he showed his hole card. That might take a little doing. He said, "All right, I'm here, Gallagher. Let's get on with it. Where are these men that you intend to turn over to my custody?"

Clem Gallagher's horse was facing west. He turned him to come alongside Longarm. He pointed and said, "Do you see way up yonder beyond that old shack? Well, there's a rise that drops off right sharp. Right below that is a *barranca,* a crevice. I've got fourteen bandits down in there who we're holding under guard who have been going around doing depredations and other bad things in my name. Every damn one of them will tell you so. I want my name cleared and I want my brother's name cleared and I want my family's name cleared."

Longarm glanced back to see how Fisher and the other man were faring. By now, they were close to a mile away, although Longarm noticed that Fisher had imperceptibly dropped back behind the other man. Not much, but just to where he had the advantage.

Longarm said, "By the way, whatever happened to your other brother, Vern?"

Gallagher's eyes narrowed to slits. He said, "Some sonofabitch blowed him all to hell just outside of Lawton. It was at Lily Gail's place. Damnedest thing that you ever saw. We had a man, a cousin by the name of Emmett, working there at that time. He came and told us that there was trouble and that we needed to come and help Lily Gail. Emmett led Vern and five or six others from the family, but they never came back, Marshal Custis Long. Everything exploded. You wouldn't know anything about that, would you?"

Longarm said evenly, "Listen, Gallagher. I'm only interested in one thing and that's what kind of a deal we can make. I don't know about your brother, I don't know about your family, I don't know about your old man that started this whole thing. All I know is that if you are as innocent as you claim you are, then you have nothing to worry about. If people have been going around committing, as you call it, depredations in your name, then we'd want to put a stop to all that, wouldn't we? So, you just lead off."

Without another word, Clem Gallagher started his horse off. He was to Longarm's left. Longarm didn't know if he had planned it that way, but it didn't seem to make any difference. As featureless as the terrain was, there was very little cover to be seen, other than the old shack.

They rode along silently. Longarm's thoughts, however, were beginning to turn to the nitroglycerin. Now it was protected by nothing but the ice in the oilskin packets. He hoped that it would be enough because by now the sun was boiling down hot enough to cook a lizard on a flat rock.

They were proceeding in a due easterly direction across the barren land. Longarm tried to keep his position slightly behind Clem Gallagher, but Gallagher seemed aware of the move and the more Longarm slowed his horse, the more Gallagher did the same, making sure they stayed abreast. Ahead and off to their right about fifty yards was the dilapidated-looking two-story house. It was bigger than the usual run of sodbusters' homesteads. Somebody with enough money to truck enough lumber by wagon to build such a place had had a try at making a living off the barren ground. He knew that about four miles further on was the town of Quitman. Very little went on there besides drinking, gambling, whoring, and fighting. It drew the worst of a bad lot of people from a fifty-mile radius. If there was one thing that the Cimarron Strip could claim no shortage of, it was riffraff, bandits, criminals, and murderers of every ilk and every description.

They were just coming opposite the old house with its sagging porch and knocked-out windowpanes when Clem Gallagher suddenly stopped his horse. Longarm looked around at him. He said, "What's going on, Gallagher?"

Gallagher spurred his horse and wheeled around to face Longarm. He said, "Well, Mister Deputy Marshal Custis Long. The famous Longarm who's been dogging our tracks for years, nipping at our heels, caused our daddy an early death, killed God knows how many kin of ours. Well, now, Mister Sonofabitch, the shoe's on the other foot and it ain't on your horse. It's fixing to be on your neck. Do you hear me?"

Longarm stared back at him. He said evenly, "I don't know what kind of hand you're playing here, Gallagher, but it's a very dangerous one, unless you're better with that revolver at your side than I think you are."

"Oh, I ain't going to need this revolver. You just glance to your right, Mister Famous Lawman. There's five rifles trained on you out from that shack you thought was deserted."

Longarm said, "Yeah, who says so?"

"Just have yourself a look."

Longarm cut his eyes ever so slightly to the right. He had no difficulty spotting the rifles suddenly protruding from the broken windows. He counted five in a swift glance. At twenty-five yards they couldn't possibly miss him.

He turned his head back to Clem Gallagher. "I expected something like this, Gallagher. That's why we have Rufus. If I'm not back in two hours, your brother is going to be hung up from an oak tree and skinned alive. Do you understand what I'm saying?"

The thin-faced man drew his lips back in what Longarm took to be some sort of a satisfied smile. "Why, you damn fool. That wasn't Rufus. That were a second cousin of ours named Jeremiah Kettle."

Longarm said slowly, "I see. So the scar on the jaw was just a coincidence. Is that right?"

"Do you mean would Miss Lily Gail deliberately lie to you? Well, I don't know about that, Longarm. Maybe she just got confused. A lot of people mistake Orvil for my brother Rufus. You ain't so very damn smart yourself. I was doing all the talking and Rufus is the elder. Do you reckon that I'd have been doing all that talking if Rufus had been there?"

"I guess I was a little slow about that."

"I reckon that you're going to be slow about a lot of things by the time we get through with you."

"Well, I'm still confused. How did Lily Gail make up a story like that so quick? You couldn't have anticipated that."

Clem Gallagher made that smile again. "That's a mighty smart little lady, Marshal Longarm. She does things real good. It appears that some of the things she does you like. Some of them other things, you don't like."

"That man is still your second cousin. You know that he'll never make it back to you."

Clem Gallagher said, "Who the hell cares? I've got more damn cousins than your mother has fleas."

"I guess you must be an expert on fleas, Gallagher. You appear to have some in your brain. Do you have any idea what's going to happen to you if you harm a deputy U.S. marshal? You think you've been hunted before? That ain't a drop in the ocean to what will happen afterwards. The entire marshals service will devote the rest of their time to running you to the ground."

Clem Gallagher spat over the side of his horse. "Who gives a damn. We ain't scared of your marshals service. Ya'll have been trying to catch us for years. You ain't done a very good job of it."

Longarm said, "I think you're lying about Rufus."

Clem laughed. He turned his head toward the house. He yelled, "Rufus! Rufus! There's a man out here that thinks you ain't here! He thinks that you went off into New Mexico Territory with that other marshal! What did you do that for?"

Longarm turned his head to the right and looked at the shack. As he did, a man wearing an identical linen duster, only taller and heavier, came walking out carrying a carbine. He, too, wore a black flat-crowned hat, but around his neck he had a red handkerchief bound to keep the dirt from getting down inside his shirt. Longarm could see that he was wearing a vest and that his pants were held by both a belt and suspenders.

Clem Gallagher said, "There's Rufus now. Why don't you ask him how much we care what happens to Orvil Kettle? You can kill the sonofabitch for all we care. We're content to have your ass. Now, I'll tell you what you can do. Just as careful as you can, step down off that horse. Don't you make no sudden move. Before you do, I want you to reach down and get ahold of your carbine with the one hand, get hold of it by the stock, pull it out, and let it fall to the ground. After that, you dismount real careful and keep both your hands in the air." As he finished his remarks, Clem Gallagher slowly drew his revolver and pointed it at Longarm. He said, "Now is that clear?"

As Longarm pulled out his carbine from the boot, he glanced to the right to where Rufus Gallagher still stood. He had come no further than the edge of the porch. He stood there watching. Longarm assumed that whatever kind of party that they had in mind for him would take place inside the shack and that Rufus was probably the chief organizer of the festivities.

Longarm slowly eased his weight onto his left stirrup and swung his right leg over, keeping one hand on the saddlehorn and the other in the air so that Clem Gallagher would have no excuse for being sudden with the revolver that he had pointed dead at Longarm.

When he was standing by the side of his horse, both hands in the air, Clem Gallagher backed his horse up a few feet and motioned with his pistol. Gallagher said, "Walk toward me. Get clear of your horse. The horse is between you and the rifles in the house."

Longarm took two steps forward so that he was just beyond the head of his horse. He thought it would be extremely funny if they suddenly fired at him, hit his horse, and blew themselves to kingdom come. Of course, since he would go up in the same explosion, it wouldn't be nearly as funny as it would be if he wasn't there.

Longarm watched as Clem Gallagher dismounted and walked toward him, his revolver in his right hand. He came and stood face-to-face with Longarm, or he came to stand in front of Longarm and tilt his face up to look into Longarm's. He was even shorter than Longarm had thought. With his left hand, Clem Gallagher reached out and took Longarm's revolver out of the holster. He pitched it to his left, toward the porch. Longarm hated to see his carefully kept weapon skidding along in the dust.

Clem Gallagher said, "Well, now, Mister Lawman. What do you think of yourself now?"

"I am supposed to stand here with my hands in the air like some damn fool? You've got me disarmed. Are you afraid of an unarmed man?"

Gallagher made a clucking sound in his voice that Longarm took for laughter. "By all means, Mister Lawman, put your hands down. You might need to scratch your ass. You might need to scratch a lot of places when we get through with you. You might not have a use for that little pistol that you use on Lily Gail so well."

Longarm said, "Let me ask you something, Gallagher." He turned before going on and looked at Rufus standing on the porch with his rifle. His rifle was hanging casually, not pointed at any one thing, but then Longarm reckoned that there were several backup rifles aimed directly at him. Whatever he did, it was going to have to be done soon and sudden. Once they got him inside the shack, they would no doubt bind his hands and then his options would be slim. He hooked his hands in his gunbelt, working his left thumb into the silver buckle where he kept the derringer. He made it seem like a casual nonchalant gesture intending to show that he wasn't afraid. He said again, "Let me ask you something, Gallagher. You've gone through a hell of a lot of trouble to get me here and I'm curious as to the reason. Is it because of all that cash and silver that you think that I'm going to stop you from robbing in Springer, or is it because old Vern went up in a million pieces?"

Gallagher's eyes suddenly blazed. He shifted the pistol to his left hand and with his right slapped Longarm with the flat of his hand as hard as he could. Longarm let the blow turn his face so that he was looking at the cabin. Then Gallagher came with a backhanded slap, only this time as the blow was carrying his face sideways, Longarm's big right arm was coming up to grab Gallagher around the neck. As he grabbed him, Longarm pivoted, changing his position to face the shack. By that time he had the derringer out in his left hand and he was holding Gallagher up against his front, squeezing him with the muscles of his right arm against the man's neck. He could hear Gallagher making choking sounds as he struggled.

On the porch, Rufus had brought up his rifle. Longarm stooped lower so that his head was not so far above Clem's.

He jabbed Gallagher hard in the back and said, "I've got a derringer in your back, boy. I've got a .38-caliber derringer, two barrels, and I'll blow your spine in two if you don't drop that revolver right now, right now, right now."

Clem Gallagher was still making the gurgling sounds. Both of his arms were held straight out in front of him. His almost nerveless fingers let the pistol slip. It fell to the ground. Longarm began to back toward his horse, crabbing sideways. He yelled at the house, "Rufus, I've got a derringer in your brother's back. You'd better put that rifle down right now or I'm going to blow the living hell out of him. Do you understand me? Put that rifle down."

Rufus Gallagher said, "You go to hell." Suddenly, with one spring, he jumped back through the open door of the shack. Gallagher tried to struggle, but Longarm clamped him tighter. By now, Longarm was at the head of his horse. He said to Clem, "Take hold of the bridle of my horse. Take hold of him right now." He jabbed him hard with the derringer.

Clem Gallagher slowly put out a hand and took hold of the reins. Longarm began to back away from the shack. Unwillingly, Clem Gallagher was forced to lead Longarm's horse. As they went backwards, someone in the house fired. Dust kicked up two or three feet to Longarm's left and a bullet went whining off.

Longarm yelled, "One more shot and I'll shoot this sonofabitch through the back."

To illustrate his point, he raised his left hand so that they could see the derringer. Then he quickly stuck it back into Clem Gallagher's spine. Little by little, they were putting some distance between them and the house.

Another rifle cracked and dust stirred under the belly of Longarm's horse. He yelled, "You better stop that shooting. One more time and I'm killing this sonofabitch."

A voice yelled back. Longarm assumed it was Rufus. The voice said, "Yeah, you kill him, then what are you going to do?"

"I'll take it one at a time," Longarm said. "But one thing that's for certain is that I'll kill your damn brother."

The voice yelled back, "Then what are you going to do, Mister Marshal? Your pistol is lying up here and your rifle is in the sand. What are you going to do to defend yourself? Throw rocks at us?"

The distance had widened to some fifty or sixty yards. Longarm said, "Take your choice. If it's worth that to kill me, ask old Clem how he feels about it."

Clem Gallagher was still making the gurgling sound. He seemed to be getting limp at the knees, and Longarm suddenly realized that he was choking the man, cutting off his wind. He eased the pressure slightly. He said, "Tell them, Clem. Tell them how you feel about swapping out your life for mine. Tell them if they ought to trade your life for mine."

At first Clem Gallagher's voice came out in a hoarse whisper, and then he cleared his throat and coughed for a moment. He said, still hoarsely, trying to shout, "Don't shoot, for heaven's sakes, don't shoot. Hell, Rufus, I'm your flesh and blood. Don't shoot. Hell, let the sonofabitch go. We'll get him another time."

Longarm clamped his arm solid around Clem Gallagher's neck. He called out, "There ain't going to be a next time."

A shot suddenly rang out and Longarm heard a thud.

Chapter 9

For a second he thought they had shot his horse, and then he felt the body go slack in his arms and he realized that they had just shot his hostage. Another shot exploded from the shack, catching the Gallagher he was holding high on the shoulder. He suddenly realized that they were aiming for the arm he had around the man's neck. By the weight of the body, he could tell the man was dead. He yelled, "Rufus, you crazy sonofabitch. Is it so important that you just killed your own brother?"

There was a loud cackle from the shack and a new voice called out, "That ain't Clem Gallagher. I'm Clem Gallagher, you ignoramus Mister Smartass U.S. Deputy Marshal. That there fool you're cuddling up to is our half-brother Virgil."

Longarm was still stumbling backwards, trying to move away from the shack as fast as he could. Then he realized that the body that he was holding was no longer leading the horse. He took two quick steps forward, switching arms as he did, and grabbed the horse's reins with his right hand, starting to run backwards, moving fast. Another shot was fired that thudded into the body. Longarm realized that very shortly they were going to hit him in the arm and probably break it. He estimated that he was some sixty to seventy-five yards from the shack. He yelled, "What kind of people are you that you'd kill your own half-brother?"

A deeper voice yelled. Longarm assumed it was Rufus. It said, "We got lots of half-brothers, but there ain't but one of you and we're kind of sick of you, do you understand? You're right, there ain't going to be no next time. This is the time."

Just as he said it, Longarm suddenly released the dead body, and sprang behind his horse, frantically trying to increase the distance. Two shots rang out, and he heard and felt the thuds into the side of his horse. Instantly, he realized that if the horse fell full out, the nitro would blow up. The horse was swaying on his legs. He had already gone down to his front knees. Bending low, Longarm worked the ties that were holding his saddlebags. With his left shoulder, he was trying to prop the horse up as more bullets hit the carcass of the poor animal. It was taking all his strength. The horse's weight was bearing down on him harder and harder. He imagined that the animal was already dead. At any second now, the horse's hind quarters would crumple and the nitro would go up, blowing him and the horse a long way up in the sky. Then, just as his strength was about to fail him, he undid the last tie and jerked the saddlebags loose. He fell at the same time as the horse, using the carcass as protection from the rifle bullets that were beginning to sing over his head.

Longarm was in no immediate danger. They could not hit him from where they were in the shack as long as he lay prone behind his horse. But all they had to do was spread either to the left or to the right, flanking him, and he was a goner. All he had in the way of a weapon was a two-shot derringer that was ineffective over five yards. There was, of course, the nitro and the slingshot, but he couldn't raise up enough to sling one of the vials into the cabin. He could, perhaps, work his way onto his back, but that would expose him if he lay in such a way that he could see the shack. If he could see them, they could see him.

Meanwhile, the occupants of the shack seemed to take pleasure in whining bullets inches over his head. Occasionally, one of the slugs would hit his saddle and bits of leather and wood would fly. He thought of his horse, and it made him angrier than anything else. He had owned the dun for a good two years and during that time, the animal had never let him down. Even dying, he had managed to stay on his feet long enough for Longarm to free his saddlebags and keep the nitro from exploding.

Longarm was in a tight place and he knew it. He couldn't run and he couldn't fight. It was only a matter of time before they got tired of playing with him, circled around out of the range of his derringer, and either killed him outright or took him prisoner and killed him at their leisure. He rather imagined that the latter would be more to their taste.

As carefully as he could, without raising his head, he slipped the slingshot and one of the oilskins containing a vial of nitro out of one side of his saddlebags. He was unpleasantly surprised to see how little ice remained. In another thirty minutes, it would all be gone and then the hot sun would start warming the nitro. He'd understood from Simmons that it didn't have to get very warm to explode. The slightest movement could set it off. If he didn't get a shot at the shack in the next five minutes, he was in fairly serious trouble. He'd been in some tight places before and had always found a way to escape, but this time he wasn't sure there was a way. At the moment, he was facing, by his best count, at least five rifles. He was behind a dead horse. He had a popgun that was a better weapon beyond five yards if you threw it. He had two vials of nitroglycerin that in the next fifteen to twenty minutes could very easily blow him sky-high unless he could find a way to use them. Other than that, the situation looked pretty good. He glanced up toward the sun. There was no hope of nightfall. Dusk was a good two hours away, and long before that the Gallaghers would figure out that he didn't have a weapon in the saddlebags that they must have seen him untie. Or they would think that it might be a weapon of such limited range that they could flank him and force his surrender.

They seemed to have an unlimited supply of ammunition, judging from the steady barrage of shots that kept zipping over his head or thudding into his dead horse or hitting his saddle or kicking up dust behind him. Pretty soon, he decided, one of them was going to get the bright idea to get on top of the roof. He calculated the man would be able to whittle off his right side. The way he was lying on his belly the angle would be just right. The only chance that he had, and it seemed to be a very slim one, was to risk slingshoting a vial of the nitro at the shack. To do it meant that he would have to expose himself for two or three seconds. The nitro wasn't something that you jerked around, so he would have to move very slowly and very carefully and with those five rifles aimed at him, it was almost a certainty that if he wasn't killed outright, he would be wounded so badly that his chances of getting medical help would be slim.

Yet he couldn't lie there and do nothing. As carefully as he could, he slid a vial of the nitro out of the oilskin pouch in the saddlebags. He took the slingshot handle in his left hand and with his right, he put the vial of nitro in the leather pouch. His hands were trembling at a time when he needed them to be rock steady. His only hope would be to roll over on his back, push out a bit from the cover of his horse, and try a blind shot at the shack. It was a very-high-odds play.

Then suddenly, he heard rifle fire from a different quarter. It was not shots coming from the cabin. In fact, the firing from the cabin had suddenly ceased. His head was near the rump of his horse and the shots were coming from the west. He inched himself forward a foot, careful of the nitro, and peered out from behind the hindquarters of his horse. A few hundred yards away, he could see a man lying in a prone position and firing. It was Fisher Lee. Longarm smiled. He said, "Fisher, you old sonofabitch, I love you."

The unexpected rifle fire on their flank had distracted the men in the shack long enough to divert their attention from Longarm. He knew he had about ten seconds and it was a do-or-die ten seconds to save his life. The distracting fire that Fisher was laying down was nothing more than that, a distraction. In the long run, he could make no difference in the outcome of the battle, and he could do nothing to save Longarm's life. He was firing from just within the perimeter of his range. He was also firing from a very exposed position, and if they chose to turn all their weapons on him, he would be an even easier target than Longarm was.

He didn't think all these things, he simply reacted as each thought raced through his mind. In an instant, he had swiveled around, come up to one knee, and with one smooth motion drew back the pouch, aiming, judging the distance, hoping he was right, calibrating as he had never calibrated a shot with any other weapon before, and then releasing the shot as he dropped down behind his horse.

For a long time, it seemed as if nothing had happened. Then there came a blast that even he could feel from where he was. Longarm wasn't waiting for the blast, nor was he wasting time attempting to see what the results of the first shot had been. From the second that he had flopped down, he had been busy getting out the eighth and last vial of nitro. By the time the boom had finished sounding, he was already raising up to fire the second shot. He was aware as he looked that the shack was almost blown apart, but the vial was away and glittering through the sunlight and he was falling back behind his horse before the full vision registered. After that, he lay and just hugged the ground.

The second boom sounded even louder than the first. Perhaps that had been because the second vial had been warmer than the first. When he'd pulled it out of the oilskin envelope, there had been no ice left. His mind had registered that fact even as he was slipping it into the leather pouch, realizing that he was cutting it mighty thin. But he had gotten it away and the explosion had occurred where it should have.

Now he just waited. There was no more rifle fire, either from the shack or from Fisher Lee, but he wasn't going to raise his head, not for a few minutes. He was going to wait and make certain. He lay there, gripping the derringer in his hand, the slingshot's usefulness finished.

He heard a shout from the west. He cautiously looked around the rump of his horse. It was Fisher Lee. He was riding toward Longarm swinging his hat in the air and yelling.

Slowly Longarm sat up. Where there had once been a dilapidated two-story ranch house-turned-shack, there was not much of anything expect a lot of scattered boards and a few bodies that he could see. Several horses were running around loose behind where the structure had been. There had obviously been a corral behind the house, and now the horses had been released. He wondered if any of them had been hurt.

Longarm slowly stood up and put the derringer in his pocket. It didn't seem to be of much use. He looked to his right as Fisher came skidding up, still whooping and yelling. Fisher had a big smile on his face. He pulled his horse to a stop and said, "Well, Longarm, you've finally made as big a bang as you've been trying to do all your life. Hot damn, that was the damnedest thing that I've ever seen in my life. Did you know that the first valentine of yours went right through the front door? I know you didn't aim, I know you were blind lucky like you were playing poker with me last night, but that thing went right through the front door. The roof lifted clean off that place. I can tell you right now, you wasted that second one. If there had been a swinging dick left standing in there, he'd have had wings and a halo, I can promise you that."

Longarm said, "Well, Fish, for some reason, I didn't want to waste the time taking a good look. Things had been a mite warm around here up until the time you showed up, so I figured that I better get that second one in there before it went off in my hand."

Fisher said, "Well, it wouldn't be the first time something went off in your hand."

Longarm came around his horse and said, "Speak for yourself, you sonofabitch. Look here, Fisher. They killed my damn horse. I paid three hundred dollars for that horse and it was a good one, too."

Fisher jerked his head westward. "They fooled us Longarm. That one with the scar on his jaw, that wasn't Rufus after all. It was a cousin of theirs by the name of Jeremiah."

"How come he told you?"

"I think he thought it was funny. He was telling me what all they were going to do to you."

"You didn't help him talk any?"

"Yeah, well, along toward the end I did."

"He still alive?"

"He might be."

"Where is he?"

"He's tied to a tree."

Longarm shook his head and laughed ruefully. "They double-dealt us in both cases. That one I thought was Clem, that wasn't Clem, it was their half-brother Virgil. They shot him, he's laying over there. I grabbed him and got my derringer in his back and was trying to make a getaway, thinking I had Clem and that I was safe, and they up and shot the sonofabitch. What do you think about that?"

Fisher looked thoughtfully at the remains of the old ranch building. "I think their double-dealing days are over with, Longarm. I think this country is now rid of the Gallaghers once and for all."

Longarm said, "Yeah, but it took long enough, didn't it? How many people did they kill and how much money did they steal and how many horses and cattle did they rustle? Hell, Fisher, I can't blame you for not wanting to be a lawman. We don't do a very good job sometimes."

Fisher said, "Oh, cut out that horseshit. You know better than that. You just did a hell of a job and you know it."

They were standing there, fifty yards away from the destroyed building. Longarm said, "You know I owe you my life, don't you?"

"We going to start talking like that? About who owes who what? We'd have to go back a long time to figure out who saved who last."

"Nevertheless, I was a cooked goose until you laid down that distracting fire. You know, that wasn't real bright, Fish. There were five rifles firing from that shack, and there were windows on the side that you were on and you were as exposed as hell. The only thing that you done was left your horse back a little. How come you had that much sense?"

Fish said, "I wasn't planning on homesteading that particular ground that I was laying on. As soon as I got off a few shots and got you some relief, I was getting out of there. You could either take advantage of it or not, but I wasn't going to stay there."

Longarm chuckled. "Well, I reckon that we ought to go up and see what there is to see, but before we do, I want to make mention of something. There is a large sum of rewards due on the Gallaghers. I'm going to certify them as killed. Most of the rewards, obviously, are dead or alive. As a deputy U.S. marshal, I am going to put you in for those rewards."

Fisher said, "That ain't quite the straight, is it, Longarm? I didn't kill or capture any of them."

Longarm answered, "As far as I am concerned, you killed Clem and Rufus with rifle power into that shack."

Fisher looked at him with rounded eyes. "You know, you're probably talking about a pretty good piece of change. There's been rewards laid up for these boys back when I was a lawman."

"I would reckon it to be around five or ten thousand dollars all told."

"Longarm, you'd better think about this."

"I don't have to think about it, Fish. I'd be rotting in the sun by now or else in their hands if you hadn't done what you did. The only thing that I ask is that when you collect the money, I want the three hundred dollars back

161

for my horse that they killed. Bastards!"

Fish said, "Longarm, you are the strangest thing that I've ever seen. I think you're about half crazy."

"You have to be. Well, come on and let's walk up there and take a look at the damage. I hate to look at men that's been blown apart, but I think that's what we're going to find. Damn, that stuff is powerful!"

"Yeah, but ain't you powerful glad you had it?"

"It turned the trick, there ain't no question about it. I think we'll have good news to give Simmons. I think he can build his railroad now and ship his ore."

"Deputy Marshal, you done good, but you still can't beat me playing poker."

"Aw, hell, Fisher. Just because you quit your job, you automatically think that you're a professional poker player. You ain't no better poker player now than when you were a sheriff."

"You just wait until we get back to Taos. I'll play you some heads-up poker when there ain't no heat on and we'll see how well you play. Hell, I was distracted, that's the only way you beat me. You sitting over there with God knows how much explosives and expecting a man to play cards."

They were walking slowly toward the shack. Longarm stopped once to pick up his revolver. He said, "Look at this. Dust up the barrel, dust in the cylinder. My God, it'll take me an hour and a half to clean this revolver."

Fisher said, "Well, that's better than having dust up your nose and dust up your mouth and dust up your ass. That's what buried people get."

"Fisher, you're an irreverent sonofabitch, did you know that?"

They continued walking toward the shack. From what

162

he was catching glimpses of, Longarm knew that he really didn't want to look at the results of his work.

They rounded up most of the horses. A few they had to shoot. Longarm picked out the best of the lot to make the ride back to Springer. He chose a big bay mare that seemed mannerly enough and reined fairly well, although the horse was not trained to his standards. He insisted on getting his own shot-up saddle from his own dead horse, even though the saddle was nearly shot to pieces. He said, "Listen, I'll carry this back to Denver with me. This saddletree was made especially for me to fit my butt. I'll take it back to the saddle maker that's been making saddles for me for twenty years and get some new leather put back on it. Those sonofabitches are not going to kill my horse *and* ruin my saddle at the same time. Do you realize they were trying to kill me, kill my horse, and ruin my saddle? Damn, that's enough to make anybody angry."

He found his carbine full of sand. That made him angry all over again, but in the end, looking at the whole picture, he had to admit to Fisher that he was pretty pleased with the way things had turned out.

They left the bodies and the parts of bodies just as they lay. They went through enough billfolds to discover that they had indeed killed the last two of the Gallagher brothers. Longarm took along their personal effects to prove that it was true.

He said, "I think we can ask Eugene to send a crew out to collect these remains. I think they'll be glad to know that they can build their railroad now without getting any more men hurt, so they ought to be willing to do it. Anyway, we ain't going to."

They collected four loose horses and drove them ahead of them as they headed back to Springer. On the way, they stopped to take Jeremiah into custody. He was considerably shocked to learn that the Gallaghers' plan hadn't worked and that he was headed for a federal prison.

Fisher said, "I probably should have killed the sonofabitch. He ain't got no idea what's in store for him at the federal prison."

Longarm grinned. "Are you trying to talk him into running, Fish?"

Jeremiah didn't think that any of the talk was funny. He was riding with his hands tied to the saddlehorn, on lead, stripped of his hat, his boots, and his shirt. Fisher said, "I thought the boy might have a more difficult time traveling if he wasn't carrying quite so many clothes."

Longarm said, "That was damned thoughtful of you."

It was a long ride to Springer, longer than Longarm had remembered taking when they came out, but they finally arrived around ten that night. He put Jeremiah in the jail with the local sheriff, and then sought out Eugene to get accommodations for himself and for Fisher for the night.

The young foreman was ecstatic at the news, and he couldn't seem to do enough to make Longarm and Fisher comfortable. Even at that late hour, he routed out a cook to make them a meal and insisted that they stay in the mining camp guest facilities rather than go to a hotel. He said, "We can beat any hotel in this town all hollow. What time will you be wanting to go back tomorrow, Marshal? Or if you'd like, I can put a special train on tonight and send you on back to Taos."

Longarm said wearily, "No, thank you, Eugene. Tomorrow around ten o'clock will suit me fine. I'm not in a rush. To tell you the truth, I'm plain bone-tired. I'd like to have a good supper, some whiskey, and sleep. Then I'd like to have a good breakfast, get on the train, and go on back, and I believe Mister Fisher Lee here concurs with me. He, by the way, is the real hero of the moment."

Fisher said, "Aw, you're just saying that because it's true, Longarm."

Longarm looked at him and shook his head. "Lord, I wish I didn't owe you so much. Now I'm going to have to put up with your sarcasm and your bragging and your know-it-all attitude for the rest of my life."

Fisher said, "Which, the way you're going, ain't going to be very long."

Chapter 10

After a late breakfast of steak and eggs, Longarm and Fisher left on the mountain train headed for Taos. They left with the thanks of Eugene and his crew and all the members of the Springer branch of the Silverado Mining Company. Their gratitude was almost embarrassing. Two of the crew had even contrived to install chairs in the stock car so that they could ride with their horses in some comfort. Eugene had, somewhere, discovered two quarts of brandy, which he gave Longarm as they were on the way out.

As the train chuffed its way out and started up into the mountains, Longarm said, "Wow, I've got to say, Fish, I'm glad that's over. If I've never got to see another drop of nitroglycerin the rest of my life, I will be just as happy. You know, it's a hell of a situation when a man is more afraid of his own weapons than he is of his enemy."

Fisher asked, "Are you just now figuring that out?"

The train wound slowly over the mountains, laboring over the high passes, until it got up above the altitude where it could begin its descent into the valley where Taos was located. After that, it was a swift trip. As they rolled along, swaying and rocking, Longarm thought of Lily Gail and wondered where she would have fled to. He had plans for her that she didn't know about. He imagined that she was going to be hard to find, but she would turn up sooner or later. After all, they had unfinished business. Fisher had seen to that with his untimely knock on the door.

Longarm felt stiff and sore. He didn't know if it was the result of the riding, climbing the butte, riding the uncomfortable train, or spending about three weeks behind his dead horse with every muscle tensed while bullets sailed over his head and the nitroglycerin percolated under his chest. He figured maybe the time behind his horse when he was trying to draw himself up into as small a parcel as possible might have caused the aches and pains. He figured he was not getting any younger, and such ventures as he had gone through weren't slowing down the aging process one bit.

They pulled into the yard at the mining company in Taos, and Longarm and Fisher got down while their horses were unloaded. He didn't know what he was going to do with the bay mare, but he figured it was his to do with as he saw fit. He and Fisher split up at the rail yard, Fisher to go to his hotel, and Longarm to go see Simmons and give him a report and thank him for all the support that the mining company had given. He left Fisher with the understanding that he would see him sometime after lunch. Fisher said, "I want a bath, another meal, maybe some sleep, and then maybe I'll be fit company."

"Well, the bath and the meal will help, but I doubt if it will help enough. I feel like a bath myself, even though we had one last night at the railroad place in Springer. I could use a clean shirt and some clean jeans."

"Well, I'll see you later then." With that, Fisher mounted his horse and rode off while Longarm stepped across the

168

tracks, leading the bay mare in the direction of Simmons's office. The distance was such that he normally would have gone on horseback, but he didn't much feel like riding the Gallaghers' horse, and besides, it felt good to stretch his legs after the cramped ride through the mountains. His mood should have been exalted. To have finally finished off the Gallaghers should have been perhaps as big an accomplishment as he had recorded to date. But something was lacking, and he rather suspected that something was the fact that he had caught them by a fluke, that if he had not gone on leave he would not have been where they could fall into his hands. But in poker, as in life, there was just no substitute for luck. What he supposed had made him the most tired was the pure fear of handling the liquid lightning. Now that it was over, he could look back and realize the chance that he had taken dealing with such a dangerous cargo with so little knowledge. He was frankly amazed that Simmons had allowed him to have it. In fact, he considered recommending to the mining engineer that in the future he be more careful who he allowed to lay hands on such undependable goods. It brought a shudder up his back as he recollected how he had transported such a commodity, how he had handled it, and how he had actually shot it with a slingshot. Well, he thought, this was one chapter in his life that should not be bandied about and become general gossip or part of the Longarm legend of tomfoolery. For that reason, he had great hopes that somehow the story would not get back to Billy Vail. Of course, he knew that somehow Billy would hear that he'd had a hand in the demise of the Gallagher brothers, but if it was possible, he was going to take every measure to make sure that Billy did not have new material with which to spur him about the head and shoulders.

As he opened the door to the office, he could tell that Eugene must have wired on ahead. The clerk immediately jumped up and ran into Simmons's office and the mining engineer came out immediately. He came forward and shook Longarm's hand over and over, telling him how grateful the mining company was for his help. They went in to the engineer's office, and Simmons proposed a toast of an elegant brandy, which Longarm was glad to get, not for the sake of the toast but for the sake of the smooth, relaxing liquor.

Simmons was going on and on about the amazing feat that Longarm had pulled off. Finally, Longarm could stand it no longer. He said, "Mister Simmons, as a law officer, I've got to warn you about something."

Simmons looked up at him alertly and said, "Yes, Marshal, what would that be?"

Longarm said, "In the future, I think you ought to be more careful about who you let lay hands on that nitro."

Simmons looked puzzled. "But I gave it only to you, no one else."

"That's my point, Mister Simmons. What the hell do I know about nitroglycerin? It could have gotten me and a lot of other people killed. I'm not responsible enough to be handling that kind of stuff."

Simmons's mouth fell open. He said, "Well, Marshal, you must understand that when a federal marshal requests something to be used in the furtherance of justice, this company and myself personally have no choice but to grant that wish. We are here under the auspices of the United States Mining Commission, who could revoke our claim at any time."

Longarm said, "Never mind that. I just want you to be a little more careful. Next time I come in here and ask you to give me some nitroglycerin, don't you do it. My nerves will never be the same after this one episode. That stuff is dangerous, Mister Simmons."

Simmons studied Longarm in amazement. "Excuse me, Marshall," he said, "do you not recollect that I gave you quite a lecture on nitro and warned you and rewarned you that transporting such an explosive was both dangerous and unwise?"

"Then you should have followed your advice and kept it the hell out of my hands."

Simmons finally had to smile. "Well, from what I hear, Marshal, you handled it properly, you handled it accurately, and you handled it effectively. I'd have to say that if your services were available as a demolition man, I wouldn't hesitate to put you to work."

Longarm took a quick hard slug of the brandy. "Mister Simmons, don't say things like that, even in jest. Sir, I today have realized the risks that I took and I have to tell you in all seriousness that right now, I'm more scared than I've ever been before in my life."

Simmons laughed. "I know how you feel, Marshal. There have been several times in my career when I have taken chances with dynamite or nitro and looked back later and wondered how I managed to stay in one piece. It is very easy to tell a man how very dangerous that stuff is, how volatile it is, but until a man has seen for himself what destruction it can cause, he doesn't really understand what he's told. I want you to know that if there is ever anything that this mining company can do for you personally, all you have to do is ask."

Longarm said, "There is one thing that you can do for me, Mister Simmons."

"Name it and you've got it."

Longarm said, "Hitched out in front of your office with my saddle on it is a horse that belonged to the Gallaghers.

171

That one and four others that we drove on ahead and the one man in jail is all that is left of them. I don't want that horse, but I can't just turn her loose. Would the mining company take that horse off my hands? By rights, you have suffered great damage at the hands of the Gallaghers, and I could easily and quite willingly turn this horse over to you as partial reparation for the damage they've done to you. We left the other horses with Eugene in Springer."

Simmons said, "Why are you riding a Gallagher horse? Where is yours, Marshal?"

Longarm looked grim. "The bastards shot it. It happened that the horse was between me and them, so they shot the horse to get to me. It was a damn good horse that I paid three hundred dollars for a couple of years ago, and he'd been a good using horse, and if anything makes me mad about this whole deal, it's the loss of that horse."

Simmons asked, "Marshal, as a general rule, what blooded horse or cross do you prefer?"

Longarm said, "I like a cross between a Morgan and a quarter horse or a quarter horse crossed with a thoroughbred."

Simmons nodded. "All right, I'll have your saddle taken off that horse and delivered to the hotel livery stable. We'll take the horse and count it as partial compensation for the damage that we have suffered. Of course, most of that damage has been covered by the insurance company, but we'll report it to them."

Longarm said, getting up, "Well, Mister Simmons, I just wanted to let you know the final outcome. Now, I'm dead tired and I'm headed down to the hotel to get some clean clothes on and then step down to the barbershop to get a haircut. We were up all night last night, and then I laid behind a horse while people tried to cut my hair for me with their rifle bullets. That does take it out of a body."

Once again, Simmons thanked Longarm and then escorted him to the door.

Longarm was standing in his hotel room, completely nude, about to rummage in his small valise and come out with a change of clothes and socks. He had a glass of Maryland whiskey in his hand, which he had been savoring, and he had taken the time to have a short washup out of the big washbasin that the hotel had provided. He was considering whether to shave himself or treat himself to a barbershop shave when he heard the sound of a key turning in the lock of his room's door. He whirled instantly and stepped to the bedside table. He set the whiskey down and put his hand on the butt of his revolver, ready to draw it from the holster.

The door opened and Lily Gail stood there, wearing a very fetching yellow frock dress, cut low in the bodice so that her creamy white skin and the beginning of the swell of her bosom showed. She started as she saw Longarm and was almost, but not quite, able to keep the surprise out of her eyes. She said, stammering, "Why . . . why . . . why, Custis. Whatever are you doing here?"

He smiled at her. "I might ask you the same question, Lily Gail, but come in and shut the door behind you. You're creating a draft."

She stepped into the room and closed and locked the door behind her. She turned to face Longarm with about ten feet separating them. She said, "I didn't expect you back . . ." She stopped. "I didn't expect you back so soon."

He smiled even more. "Yeah, I bet you didn't."

She said, trying to keep the bewilderment out of her eyes, "Didn't ya'll get together?"

"You mean me and the Gallaghers?"

"Why, yes. Isn't that who you were going to see?"

173

"Yes, but it just didn't come off, Lily Gail. We missed connections somewhere along the line. Somebody got the time and place wrong. They never showed up."

A little of the concern left her face. She said, "Oh, well, that's too bad, but I'm sure there'll be another chance."

He said, with a smile fixed on his face, "Yeah, there's always another chance."

She walked slowly toward him. The glint that he liked so much was back in her eyes. She said, "Oh, my. Look at you. Don't you look perfect?" She came up, stood next to him, and reached down and began to fondle his member and his testicles. She said, "Oh, that's so nice."

With fingers that were trembling as they did when he handled the nitroglycerin, he began unbuttoning the convenient front of her dress. Because of the low cut, there weren't so many buttons. In less than a minute, her dress had fallen to the floor. He backed her to the edge of the bed, and she sat down and leaned forward and took him in her mouth. He put his hands on her head and held on while she wrapped her arms around his waist and pulled him back and forth into her mouth. After a few strokes, it was all he could do to hold himself back. For a second, she pulled her head away and looked up at him, running her plump tongue around her lips, and then took him back into her mouth. He could stand it for only a moment longer, and then he pulled away and pushed her back on the bed. He said, "Turn over and back up to me. Get on your hands and knees." His voice was husky as his throat began to close and his breathing quickened. The blood was pounding in his ears. She turned slowly, bringing herself to the right height. He moved forward and his member went into her, almost as if it had a mind of its own. She was slick and warm and he leaned over her, reaching under and grasping each of her breasts as he began to pump into her. He could feel himself rising and could feel the thunder inside. He heard a loud gasping and realized it was coming from him before he exploded. He felt like his whole body was being sucked into her. The explosion lasted a long, long, long time.

When it was over, he collapsed on her back. Her arms gave and her legs spread and they lay flat on the bed. They remained that way for a long moment until he regained his breath. He rolled over and lay there staring at the ceiling.

She turned and hovered over him, kissing him on the mouth. She said, "There. Wasn't that a nice welcome home."

Still out of breath, he said, "Oh, my, Lily Gail. That really was."

Then he heaved himself up. She said, "Where are you going?"

He said, "I've got to get dressed and you'd better get dressed. We've got to go out."

She asked, "Oh, where are we going?"

He said, "Well, I may be going several different places but you're going to jail. You're under arrest."

Longarm was having trouble getting her out of the room. She was saying, "But you can't arrest me, Longarm. Not after what we just done, you can't do it."

"I am arresting you, Lily Gail. I'm arresting you for complicity in the attempted murder of a federal law officer. That's officially. That's a pretty serious charge, Lily Gail, and I don't think that you're going to enjoy federal prison, but that's where you are going. This is the second time that you've nearly gotten me killed. The first time it was my fault. This time it was your fault. I'm not going to give you a chance at another try. Next time you might succeed."

She put her hand to her mouth. She said, with a break in her voice, "But honey, how can you after what you just done to me?"

He said, "What I just did to you was what you tried to do to me, sending me out to meet with the Gallaghers. Only I enjoyed mine. I don't think you're going to enjoy yours."

"How can you say that!"

"By the way, Rufus and Clem have gone to be with Vern and the rest of that sorry family."

She said, "You don't mean . . ."

He nodded. "Yes, Lily Gail. They are blowed-up suckers. Literally and figuratively. You have lost your soft touch."

As if she hadn't heard him, she said, trying to melt against him, "You can't arrest me after what we just did. You love it too much."

He said grimly, "That's just the reason, Lily Gail. I've got to put you out of my reach. You've got a power over me that I don't like. That thing that you've got between your legs is more dangerous than any gun I've ever been up against, so yes, I'm fixing to stick you in jail."

She almost wailed. "But you *can't!*"

He took her firmly by the arm and led her through the door. He said, "You watch me."

Over her protests, he marched her firmly down the street to the sheriff's jail. As they went, they created a wake of people turning to stare after them. Longarm had neglected to put on his badge, so it occurred to him that he appeared like a man dragging a woman somewhere against her will. He reached in his pocket and hooked his badge where it would be obvious.

They turned in at the jail. The outer office was empty except for one deputy. Longarm said, "I'm Deputy U.S.

Marshal Custis Long out of the Denver office. This young woman is under arrest on a serious charge. I want you to hold her in a cell while I tend to some business. I've got to say adios to an old friend, pick up some tickets for the evening train, and then get my gear and saddle. I'll be back in an hour, maybe an hour and a half. I want you to watch her, she's pretty damn slippery."

The young deputy had arisen from behind the desk when they came in. He stood there, openmouthed, staring first at Longarm's badge and then at the much more appealing sight of Lily Gail Baxter. He stammered out, "You mean, you want me to put this . . . this . . . this young lady in a jail cell?"

"Preferably one with two locks."

The young deputy said, "Well, yes, sir. If them are your orders, Marshal."

"Them are my orders. What's your name, son?"

"Clinton Watts, sir. I'm a new deputy here."

Longarm said, "Well, Deputy Watts, you see to it. I'll be back anywhere from an hour to two hours."

With that, he turned on his heels and walked out of the door, first to find Fish, then to go to the railroad station, and then finally to pay his hotel bill and get the rest of his gear.

It was an easy parting for Fisher, for they would be seeing each other soon enough since Fisher had plans to be in Denver within the next couple of weeks. Longarm reassured him that he was going to put Fisher in for the reward money. He said, "Hell, Fisher. Somebody deserves it, and you damn sure rode into the eye of the storm and did your part. I wish like hell I could collect it."

Fisher said, "We could split it."

Longarm shook his head ruefully. "No, I can't let myself do that, but I damn sure can collect three hundred of it for that horse. That makes me mad all over."

"Well, you took that bay."

"No, I gave that to Simmons. I didn't like the thought of riding a Gallagher horse."

Fisher shook his head and laughed. "Longarm, you're as crazy as hell, do you know that?"

"So they keep telling me."

After that, Longarm went to the train depot and bought two tickets for Denver. Since he didn't have a horse, he bought chair coach tickets, though he hated riding in the coach, preferring to ride back in the stock car with his animal. He went back to the hotel and paid his reckoning for his stay there. Then there was nothing to do but sling his battered saddle over his shoulder, collect his valise, and with his carbine in one hand and his saddlebags over his shoulder, head out of the hotel and back down to the jail. He only had half an hour to catch the train since he and Fisher had spent more time talking than he had reckoned. He was somewhat surprised to see the young deputy emerging through the door that led back to the cell area. The deputy was buttoning his pants and buckling his belt.

Longarm suddenly had a sinking feeling. He said, "Deputy Watts, fetch out my prisoner. I'm ready to go."

The young man's face went scarlet. He said stammering, "Uh . . . sir . . . uh . . . Marshal. She ain't here."

Longarm took a few steps toward the deputy. "What the hell do you mean, she ain't here? Where is she?"

The deputy cut his eyes back and forth. "Well, the truth of the matter is, sir, the fact of the business is . . . well, she got loose from me just now and just ran out of here. I'm the only one on duty and I'm not supposed to leave the office."

Longarm almost slapped him. "Boy, don't come out from back there licking cream off your whiskers and tell me that you've been branding cattle. I know exactly how she got out of here. Deputy, you're under arrest."

The young deputy took a step backwards. He said, "What?"

"That's right. You're under arrest for interference with a federal officer in pursuit of his duty. Trust me, young man, that's a serious offense. Hand me your side arm."

The deputy swallowed. He said, "Sir, I ain't got one. You ain't supposed to go back to the cells with a gun."

"Then it's just as well. Open that damn door behind you." With the door open, Longarm marched the deputy back into an empty cell before he slammed the door and stood there holding the keys. He said, "You are under arrest. I don't know how long I will be gone, a day, two days, two weeks, I don't know. You damn well better be in this cell when I get back or else I'll hunt you all over the world because I don't ever let anyone get away from me. Do you understand that? Your next stop is going to be about five minutes in a federal court and then you're going to be doing about ten years at Leavenworth if you get out of this cell. Understand?"

The deputy was white-faced. He said, "Marshal, please. It was more than I could take."

Longarm said dryly, "Don't tell me about her, son, I know all about her. I'm telling you once again, Deputy, that you better be in this cell when I get back."

"What if the sheriff lets me out?"

"Then tell the sheriff that I'm liable to arrest him."

The deputy swallowed and said, "Yes, sir."

Longarm turned around, walked out of the cell block and through the door, pitched the keys to the cells onto a handy desk, and then left the office. He was almost, but not quite, smiling. He wondered how long the deputy would stay in the cell. Probably a couple of days at least. He sighed. You had to hand it to Lily Gail. She was a handful and just as slippery as anything he had ever gotten his hands on.

He didn't have time to dwell on such matters. He had a train to catch. He shouldered his gear and hurried out the door and down to the depot, where he could hear the train blowing the five-minute warning.

It was three days after Longarm got back to Denver before he went into the office. He spent the time resting at his boardinghouse, drinking at his favorite saloon, playing at some cards, and paying court to a young widowed dressmaker, trying to convince her that a man and a woman didn't necessarily have to be married to enjoy each other's company to its fullest extent. He still hadn't convinced her.

On the fourth morning, he went to the Federal Building, walked into Billy Vail's office, and flopped down. His silver-haired boss tried to look astonished. He said, "Why, Longarm. What in hell are you doing back here?" He looked at a calendar. "It's only been thirteen or fourteen days of your thirty-day leave. What are you doing here?"

He knew Billy Vail already was aware of what had happened. He said, "I couldn't take no more leave time. It was wearing me out, so I figured that I had to come back to work so that I could get some rest."

"Well, are you officially reporting back to duty?"

"Not today, maybe tomorrow."

Billy Vail said, "Well, I just want to get the straight of it. You never can tell when I might be needing an extra hand. Things have been pretty quiet around here, but you never can tell when they might *blow up.*"

Longarm looked at him suspiciously, but there was nothing in his face to go on, so he let it pass.

Longarm said, "Well, I'm glad to hear that, Billy. I wouldn't want anything getting you upset."

Billy said, "I had some good news about the Gallaghers. Sounds like you did a dynamite job."

Longarm looked at him again. He said, "A what?"

Billy said, "I meant just a real fine job. Sounds like you were a real *firecracker* down there tending to the Gallaghers. I know that everybody is mighty glad and grateful for the work you done. I hear that you had a little help from a gentleman named Fisher Lee. That's an old friend of yours, ain't it?"

"Yeah."

"Guess he'll be claiming the reward money with you not being able to."

"Yeah." Longarm got up. "I just stopped by for a moment to let you know that I was back in town. I'll probably be back to work tomorrow." He started for the door.

Billy Vail said, "Oh, by the way. An odd situation happened."

"What was that?"

"The Silverado Mining Company sent a really fine horse up here for you. Must have been a thousand-dollar horse, part thoroughbred, part quarter horse. Prettiest horse that I've ever seen."

Longarm turned back quickly. "They did?"

"Yeah, and there was a letter that came with it from a Mister Simmons, the manager of their operations there at Taos. He said they wanted to give you that horse in gratitude for what you did for them."

"Well, where's the horse?"

Billy Vail attempted to look shocked. "Why, he's in government custody, Longarm. You know that you can't

181

accept gifts in your official capacity as a deputy United States marshal."

Longarm said, "But them damn Gallaghers killed my horse. I'm out a horse."

"Was that one of your personal horses?"

"Of course it was. You know that I don't ride those damn hides that we're supposed to requisition from the army."

Billy Vail shook his head. "That's too bad, Longarm. You shouldn't have been using your own personal horse in a dangerous situation like that."

"Well, how come I can't have that horse they sent me to replace the one I lost? Besides that, I gave them one of the Gallagher horses."

Billy Vail nodded. "That was all explained in the letter from Mister Simmons, and I feel really bad about the fact that you can't have this horse. It's truly a fine horse, a four-year-old gelding, a wonderful-looking animal."

Longarm gave him a disgusted look. "Aw, Billy, can't you bend the rules a little bit? Hell, this is the worst damn vacation I've ever had. I wound up working the biggest part of it, lost a good horse, nearly got myself killed. Looks like you could bend the rules a little."

Longarm did not expect compliments for what he had done to the Gallagher gang. As Billy would have said, "Hell, that's just part of your job. That's what you get paid for. Do you want pay and compliments both?" So Longarm knew better than to mention busting up the worst gang of cutthroats and crooks that the Southwest had ever seen, but he did think that he should have the horse to replace the one that he had lost.

Billy Vail said, "I know that you worked on your vacation and I know what you done. It was all in that letter that I received from Mister Simmons, and I hate it that you can't have that horse because I have the most wonderful name for it. Want to hear it?"

"Hell, no. What the hell do I care what the name of the horse is if I can't have it? Where is the horse anyway?"

"Well, I don't know, Longarm. It's the property of the United States Government, so I turned it over to the Quartermaster Corps."

Longarm stared at him in amazement. "You turned over a fine animal like that to the damn Quartermaster Corps? Billy Vail, you can make me madder than anyone that I've ever known before in my life. I thought I was mad before I came into this office, but now I am really angry." Longarm got to his feet and started for the door.

Behind him, Billy Vail said sweetly, "Wait a minute, Longarm. Don't you want to know the name that I picked out for the horse?"

Longarm took hold of the knob of the door. He said, "No."

"Well, I'm going to tell you anyway because it's perfect, it suits you."

Longarm turned and gave him a look. "All right, what?"

Billy Vail said, "Nitroglycerin. Fits you to a T. *Explosive*."

Longarm didn't bother to answer. His face reddened and his hand shook. He said, "Billy Vail, you are the worst sonofabitch that I've ever met in my life." Then he went through the door, started to close it, changed his mind, and stuck his head back in. He said, "I take that back, Billy Vail. You ain't the worst sonofabitch I've ever met because I ain't met every sonofabitch yet. You're the worst sonofabitch period."

With that, Longarm slammed the door as hard as he could, making the glass shiver. He wished it had broken.

Now there was nothing left to do but walk on out of the building and go find the saloon and a poker game and perhaps, tonight, make better progress with the lady dressmaker. Maybe he could find a loose thread on her somewhere, one that he could unravel, and get after it. He doubted it, though, the way his luck was running.

He took no great excitement in bringing the Gallaghers to book because about that he felt the same way as Billy Vail. It was his job. If a man did his job well and got paid, it was a standoff, a square deal, and that was all he had ever looked for in life. He was a little rank that day, but he knew that the next day he'd be halfway hoping that Billy Vail would summon him to the office and say, "Now, Longarm, we've got some trouble down in Texas and I reckon you're the only man for the job."

And he'd say, "Billy, you are full of it. There's half a dozen other deputies. Send one of them."

But of course, in the end, he would go because that was his job. All he wondered was how long it would take for the nitroglycerin business to blow over.

Watch for

LONGARM AND THE DEADLY THAW

198th novel in the bold LONGARM series
from Jove

Coming in June!

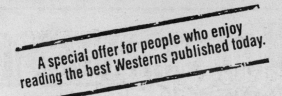

Explore the exciting Old West with one of the men who made it wild!